P9-DWZ-652

DATE DUE

THE SECOND
SCROLL

A. M. KLEIN
THE SECOND SCROLL

Introduction by Sidney Feshbach

*. . . And ask a Talmudist what ails the
modesty of his marginal Keri that Moses
and all the prophets cannot persuade him
to pronounce the textual Chetiv.*
    —JOHN MILTON

THE MARLBORO PRESS
MARLBORO, VERMONT
1985

Originally published in 1951
by Alfred A. Knopf
Copyright © 1985 by The Marlboro Press
Manufactured in the United States of America
Library of Congress Catalog Card Number 85-61442
ISBN 0-910395-15-2

REBONO SHEL OLAM:

'Tis a Thou-song I will sing Thee—

Thou . . . Thou . . . Thou . . . Thou

AYEH EMTZOEKO, V'AYEH LO EMTZOEKO?

O, where shall I find Thee? And where art Thou not
to be found?

Wherever I fare—Thou!

Or here, or there—Thou!

Only Thou! None but Thou! Again, Thou! And still,
Thou!

—RABBI LEVI YITSCHAK OF BERDICHEV

CONTENTS

INTRODUCTION

Abraham Moses Klein, 1909-1972: an extraordinary poet, who at eighteen published five sonnets on Purim in the *Menorah Journal*; a brilliant novelist, who modeled his only-published novel after the Pentateuch and its glosses; an editor, who wrote hundreds of pages of editorials over decades of the *Canadian Jewish Chronicle*; a Socialist who ran for public office in Quebec and lost; a speechwriter for Samuel Bronfman, who was the chairman of the Canadian Jewish Congress and the president of Seagrams; a scholar and critic of James Joyce's *Ulysses* . . .; a lawyer . . .; a husband and father. . . .

This remarkable range of activities was based on a private life common to many East-European Jewish immigrants and their children. Klein was born in Ratno, in north-west Ukraine — in a line on the map with Brest-Litovsk, Chelm, and Warsaw; his father, who sold pottery in Ratno, became a presser in the garment industry in Montreal; his parents kept kosher; and he went to Talmud Torah, where he studied everything from the Hebrew aleph-beth to advanced rabbinical theology.

But his Jewish Montreal was not, for example, New York City and the Lower East Side. In Montreal, the Jewish quarter was between the English Protestant and French Catholic sections, which tended to polarize into richer and poorer, federalist and separatist, powerful and powerless, indifferent anti-Semitism and overt hostility. Canada's schools were "confessional" (varieties of Christian), and Jewish children went to the Protestant school. In Klein's years, Montreal's small Jewish population expanded exponentially: 1901, about 7,000; 1921, 46,000; 1941, 64,000; 1961, 102,000; 1971, 109,000. Klein was in the first graduating class of the new Baron Byng High School, whose students were mostly Jewish; he and his co-valedictorian, Bessie Kozlow, married. He was an undergraduate at McGill University, which had an unstated quota for Jews; and he went to the University of Montreal for law. The Kleins had three children. Klein was a Zionist, approximately after the programme of Achad Ha'am.

The lives of the multiplying Montreal Jews,

Klein among them, combined dedication to Jewish identity, with its full range of differences, and a complicated in-between marginality with regard to languages, politics, schooling, and culture — all of which is being re-defined today in Francophone Quebec Province. One spectacular result of living in this in-between place is Klein's ecumenical synthesizing polyglot poem, "Montreal," beginning, "O city metropole, isle riverain/Your ancient pavages and sainted routs/Traverse my spirit's conjured avenues!/Splendor erablic of your promenades. . . ."

The University of Toronto Press is engaged in publishing a well-designed mutivolume edition —with introduction, glossaries, and archival information — of Klein's Collected Works. In print, at this time, are *Beyond Sambation: Selected Essays and Editorials 1928-1955*, edited by M. W. Steinberg. Klein's papers are in the Public Archives of Canada; the A. M. Klein Research and Publication Committee is guiding the publication of the Collected Works; Klein's biography, *Like One That Dreamed*, by the scholar and archivist, Usher Caplan, published in Canada by McGraw-Hill Ryerson, is a necessary adjunct to the works. The novel, *The Second Scroll*, has not yet appeared in the Collected Works and has not been available in the United States in decades.

Klein's first interest was poetry; he wrote in every traditional lyric form — light verse, witty and sentimental quatrains, sonnets, longer ballads, satires, psalms — and scattered throughout are some poems of extraordinary personal and general power that I find get stronger with each re-reading. For example: "Psalm 172: a Psalm of Abraham, Praying a Green Old Age":

> I who have expiated life in cities,
> Whose lungs have inhaled dust and noisome
>   oils,
> Whose ears have heard no bird's or cricket's
>   ditties,
> Whose eyes have only surmised fruitful
>   soils,
>
> I who have merely guessed the bird's
>   existence
> By sparrow-droppings on the brim of a
>   hat,
> I am that one who now, with meek
>   persistence
> Pray humbly to the Lord of Eden, that
>
> I may in such green sunny places pass
> The ultimate years that when at last I leave,
> My shoes be smooth with unguent of
>   crushed grass
> And green be on the elbow of my sleeve.

This contains several of Klein's best qualities: his constant desire to continue and to re-create Hebrew tradition in the modern world (by writing a new psalm and in his own name), his attention to lives lived in particular trying circumstances (aging in cities, not Eden), his humor (playing with a pious "His eye is on the sparrow"), his modest familiarity (a hat, shoes, sleeve), his echoes of literature (Whitman's "I lean and loafe at my ease," and his own *Hath Not a Jew*, and Shakespeare's Shylock), his witty and histrionic logic (inferrring from effect to cause), and his archaic language ("expiated," "noisome," "unguent of").

Klein's poems have a prose parallel in *Beyond Sambation*. Editor of *The Judaean*, 1928-1932, then a contributor and editor of the *Canadian Jewish Chronicle*, 1938-1955, his editorials contain a record of Canadian Jews struggling with the uncertain news of horrors in Europe, organizing to help, and responding to that historical reversal in the establishment of Israel. The editorials are also a record of this poet, who, from the first, placed every immediate event in the broad sweep of Jewish history and the linguistic resources of the many "dialects" of English literature from Chaucer to Joyce. If *Beyond Sambation* were only a limited record of Canadian Judaism, it might be restricted in interest, but, because of

Klein's idiosyncratic perspectives and inventions, it is also a chart of the vital signs of contemporary Judaism in the Diaspora, of world politics, and of himself, a remarkable poet.

Take, for example, an ordinary editorial, that of 13 March 1942: "A Great Talmudist — Rabbi Pinchas Hirschsprung Interviewed." Klein starts with a reference (in a neo-logism, made from the hated tyrant "Haman" and "maniac") to the effects of the "Hamaniac" Nazis on Europe's physical and cultural character, then on Jewish life; the resultant movement of rabbis and scholars into Canada he compares (surely, with ambivalence) with the migrations that caused the European Renaissance. He notes the twenty-seven-year-old rabbi has memorized the eighteen volumes of the Talmud and need not declare them at Customs. He explains the page layout of the Talmud, ending the paragraph with "Well has the Talmud been called a Hansard of Jewish spiritual life." The Hansard is the "official reports of the proceedings and debates of Parliament." In that small metaphor, Klein has dramatized the history and contents of the Talmud, and with a nice joke, too. He compares the rabbi with another rabbi important enough to himself to praise in a poem and to use as character in *The Second Scroll*; therefore, this comparison is typically personal and honorific. He concludes with a fuller description of the characteristics of this new rabbi — and his appointment at a synagogue. So many of these editorials have the associative flow of letters to friends, of prose-poems, of dialectical *pilpuls* shaped as monologues. Reading this editorial in 1984: after recalling, through Klein's words, the painful events of 1942, I am moved at how complex and wondrous Klein's spirit was that found light in and made light of such days of evil. *Beyond Sambation* is both topical and intriguing beyond its time.

The Second Scroll, my favorite of Klein's writings, is a masterwork of subdued power, like Sabbath cooking, simmering steadily, never brought to boil, in odor perfect and in potential a familiar feast. In it, in a fusion of his own life and writing, Klein joins his own actual trip to Israel to that of a Klein-like narrator. The narrator, a journalist-poet-Zionist, tells of his trip to Israel and his search for an uncle. The uncle, with a messianic name, Melech Davidson (King David Son), survives the 1915 pogrom in Ratno, suffers then an ideological transformation, joins the Communists after the Russian Revolution, and travels to Rome, Casablanca, and Safed. He settles in Israel, and just as he is about to be found by the nephew-narrator, Uncle Melech is murdered.

To explain Klein's title and construction I can't do better than quote from his own summary: "I wrote this book with several intentions, technical and ideological, in mind. I desired, first of all, a record, a memento of my pilgrimage, a scripture to witness to the fact that I had beheld the glory of the Jewish State's beginning, the consolation of our people's rescue.... I was struck, furthermore, by the similarity between contemporary Jewish history and our ancient saga — I thought I saw in the events of today a recurrence, in large outline, of the events recorded in the Pentateuch. This is a *Second Scroll*.... The chapters therefore follow the Mosaic sequence: *Genesis*, for obvious reason [about childhood in Montreal]; *Exodus*, likewise [about his departure for Israel]; *Leviticus*, the book concerned with priestly things, wherefore Rome, and the Monsignor; *Numbers* — because of the milling multitudes of the wider Egypt; and finally *Deuteronomy*, that is to say the recapitulation: Israel. And since no Jew can conceive of a Pentateuch without commentary — the glosses [which I see as more analogous to Haftorah or Zohar portions than Midrashic commentary]. These serve a double purpose; they repeat in minor the major themes; and they elaborate the tale's essential meaning without impeding its action."

The Second Scroll is a second naming, or deuteronomy, in several ways: the murder and burial of Uncle Melech, occuring in the *Deuter-*

onomy chapter, is a "deuteronomy" of the reburial of Theodor Herzl in Israel, of the murder of the 12th-century "returning" Judah Ha-Levi, and of the Deuteronomic blessing and death of Moses. Uncle Melech's murder and funeral are congruent also with the last of the weekly readings of the Torah and Haftorah; after this, it implies, is the immediate return to the first chapter of the novel, *Genesis*, and to the beginning of the First Scroll. And, as Klein wrote, the glosses "repeat in minor the major themes."

Klein's deuteronomic writing (his interpreting recent or present history as a renewal of the First Scroll, as a prediction fulfilled, and as an intensely personal, yet larger group experience) makes *The Second Scroll* a secular, artistic, truly-Kierkegaardian repetition: the present is, in Kierkegaard's terms, remembered forward from the First Scroll. Klein "repeats" in a lived unity ancient Israel and modern, messiah and Melech and nation, the narrator's life and his own, etc. Each moment in the novel projects exchanges between eternity and time, transcendence and immanence, past and present. Clearly, Klein intended a complex dialectics. Perhaps unsought for, but extremely important nevertheless, are the unstated tensions between the narrator's safety in peripheral Canada, the anguish, physical and spiritual, in Central Europe, and the uncertainties of spiritual and political Israel.

At the time of writing his novel, Klein was aware of Martin Buber's basic work, *I and Thou*. On December 21, 1951, Klein published an editorial cautioning Buber against accepting the Goethe Prize from the German government. "Here, too," he writes to Buber and the readers, "Buber's philosophy is pertinent and receives a mundane interpretation; it is the 'You-They' philosophy; remember who 'you' are, remember who 'they' are." Gretl K. Fischer, in her *In Search of Jerusalem: Religion and Ethics in the Writings of A. M. Klein,* finds in the novel indirect reflections of Buber's theology of a human "I," a divine "Thou," and a divinized nature. His work does reflect Buber's ideas; but with regard to Klein's artistic, not religious, interests, it is important to maintain emphasis on the "mundane," the literal (before turning to the allegorical-moral) elements. Klein had concern for the adaptation of language to concrete social needs and, in particular, to carrying out the imperative to overcome alienation and war. The novel dramatizes the relations of the "human" nephew ("I"), who speaks towards the "human" uncle ("Thou"), who, though never seen and never met, is, or was, present in certain cities — Ratno, Rome, Casablanca, Safed — each with its life — and prose-style — and who sends messages (letters, poems) that eventually reach the narrator (in the glosses). The novel contains both a physical quest and one voice seeking response from a second in dialogue. And if we neglect the "mundane," lost in some moral schematic will be the novel's mishmash of autobiography, history, and fiction. Active in *The Second Scroll* is Klein's concrete experience in Montreal of, as I wrote before, his "in-between marginality." Once again, just as Buber has stressed the dialogue of "I" and "Thou," he has meditated on the relationships, on the state of "in-between." Klein's fiction is in the tradition of Jewish rhetorical humanism, with a strong stress on oratory, litigation, and teaching, but it is motivated by a romantic intensity — that, for example, of Buber.

Klein was much influenced by James Joyce. His Talmudic training prepared him for the linguistic complexity of *Ulysses* and the products of Joyce's Jesuit training. Klein's studies of three chapters of *Ulysses*, which were written around the time of writing his novel, give evidence of the skills of the Talmudist applied to a secular work and a secular end. Miriam Waddington, in her book, *A.M. Klein*, points out some of the resemblances between the nephew and the uncle and Stephen Dedalus and Leopold Bloom, and their respective quests. To these I would add the parallel of the Mediterranean cities visited by the nephew and the uncle and the "Mediterranean" streets in *Ulysses'* Dublin. The biblical tradition that is the basis of Bloom's images of Molly Bloom is the same for the bride Jerusalem or Israel of Klein's novel. And as *Ulysses* has different styles for each chapter, *The Second Scroll* has, in the glosses, different styles and genres for each city and each chapter. The parallels are many; the differences provocative.

Yet I believe behind the fireworks of Klein's intercontinental and ontological dialectics (between Europe and Canada and Israel and between man and man and God and Man) and behind his rhetorical humanism was a simpler single profound desire to unite in his poetry his traditional Judaism re-created and the best values of Canadian democracy. Today, July 4, 1984, is the fiftieth anniversary of the death of Chaim Nachman Bialik, and tomorrow is the eightieth of Theodor Herzl's. Klein wrote, in 1953, "It was the month of Tammuz — 'Tammuz yearly wounded' — which marked the ending of both careers. . . ." He suggested Herzl, the politician, had a poetic impulse, and Bialik, the poet, had a political impulse: these led to a dialectic of possibilities and failures. "Bialik a statesman unheeded, Herzl, a poet *manqué*, the two titans of the Hebrew renascence, merge under analysis into a single colossal figure." Klein, in a poem imagining himself drowning, has appear before him his past life: "The image of myself intent/on several freedoms." This self-image includes moments in the long history of Jews searching for freedom; and his "body rises/And finds the good, the last shore!" That shore of freedom is Israel, is Paradise, and could be Canada—except . . . except that Klein had begun to feel himself a poet unheeded and a statesman *manqué*. And early in the 1950s, at the peak of productivity and recognition Klein became depressed and suicidal — to live his remaining fifteen years, in effect, a patient in his own home, tended by his wife and children and visited by a few friends. The causes of his mental and physical decline are not known, or are not known to me. Once, I thought I understood better, that Klein, like Uncle Melech, who was murdered, was "a kind of mirror, an *aspaklaria*, of the events of his own time," a mirror, though, fractured by the images it reflected. But now, with so much more of Klein's writings and his biography to read, I am less confident of an answer.

For the reprinting of *The Second Scroll*, I want to acknowledge the help of several people: Irving Layton, poet and friend of Klein, who wrote to me many years ago to tell me what was happening to Klein's health; Usher Caplan, author of the biography mentioned in this introduction, who has kept me informed about Klein scholarly activities; Zailig Pollock, the current chairman of the A. M. Klein Research and Publications Committee, who tried to sort out many frustrating. copyright confusions; Alan Kaufman, publisher and editor of the now-defunct *Jewish Arts Quarterly*, who published my first essay on Klein; Morris U. Schappes, publisher and editor of *Jewish Currents*, who has a long-standing interest in Klein and accepted a version of this introduction for his journal and gave me permission to publish it here; David and Janet Soyer, who put a copy of the novel in the hands of the director of The Marlboro Press, Austryn Wainhouse; and Oriole, who drew the thread through these many beads and more than any one person made possible something I have desired for more than twenty years — to make available to more readers A.M. Klein's *The Second Scroll*.

—SIDNEY FESHBACH

City College: CUNY
Revised, 1985

THE SECOND
SCROLL

GENESIS

F OR many years my father—may he dwell in a bright Eden!—refused to permit in his presence even the mention of that person's name. The mere imminence of an allusion to my uncle soon brought my father to an oblique deliberative ominous knuckle combing of his beard, a somber knitting of his brow, and froze at last his face to the stony stare Semitic. The tabu was recognized, and the subject was dropped.

Not that my father was by nature a furious man; he was, as a matter of fact, kind and gentle and of a very forgiving disposition; but on this question he was adamant, as unappeasable, as zealous for the Law, as was the Bible's fanatic Phineas. It was not necessary, he said, that in his house, which was by God's grace a Jewish house, there should be jabber and gossip about "the renegade," "that issuer to a bad end"; in our family we had names better distinguished with which to adorn conversation; we didn't have to be reminded of the branch lopped from the tree; the children could attune their ears to seemlier discourse; and—let it be God who judged him.

At this everyone would fall into a reminiscent sad silence, particularly my mother, who would brood awhile on the fate of her younger brother, and then, banishing willfully her unhappy thoughts, would fix the wisp of hair errant from beneath her perruque and would rise to serve tea, in glasses, each with its floating moon of sliced lemon.

My uncle's name had not always been so unwelcome beneath my father's roof. I remember well how important a part, a magic incantatory part, his name played in the early days of my childhood. I was making my first acquaintance with the letters of the Hebrew alphabet—the old Tannenbaum, round little pygmy of eighty, bearded to the breastbone, was my teacher—and I recall how it was his custom, as I struggled with the vowel-signs—those beneath the letters, like prompters prompting, and those beside the letters, like nudgers nudging, and those on top, like whisperers whispering—how it was his custom to encourage me forward from each mystic block to the next with repeated promise of pennies from heaven. The angel who presided over my lesson, he would say, would drop down candy-money if I did my lesson well. The angel kept his word, of course, and as his unseen coins suddenly hit and twirled on the big-lettered page, my mother would sigh, and exclaim: "Oh, that he might be like his uncle Melech, a scholar in Israel!"

I never saw my uncle Melech, but reports of his Talmudic exploits kept sounding in our house and there made a legend of his name. To Montreal, to our modest address on the Avenue de l'Hôtel de Ville, there came from Volhynia letter after letter, penned in the strange script of eastern Europe—all the sevens wore collars—letters twittering the praises of the young man who at the age of twenty had already astounded with his erudition the most learned rabbis of the Continent. Dubbed *the Ilui*—the prodigy of Ratno—it was in these epistles written of him, amidst a clucking of exclamation-marks, that he had completely weathered the ocean of the Talmud, knew all its bays and inlets, had succeeded in quelling some of its most tempestuous commentators; that one had not imagined that in these latter days it were possible that such a giant of the Law should arise, one had not thought that one so young could possibly excel sages twice and thrice and four times his age; but the fact was none the less incontestable that the most venerable scholars, men as full of Torah as is the pomegranate of seeds, did time and again concede him the crown, declaring that he was indeed as his name indicated, Melech, king.

Nor was he, as are so many of the subtle-scholarly, any the less pious for his learning. The six hundred and thirteen injunctions of Holy Writ, or at least those that remained binding and observable in the lands of the Diaspora, he sedulously observed; punctilious he was in his ritual ablutions; and in his praying, a flame tonguing its way to the full fire of God. He was removed from worldly matters: not the least of his praises was that he knew not to identify the countenances on coins.

My parents were very proud of him. He represented a consoling contrast to the crass loutish life about us where piety was scorned as superstition, and learning reviled as hapless, and where Jews were not ashamed to wax rich selling pork. This last was a barb aimed by my father at his cousin, a man of religious pretensions, yet by trade a pork-vender, whom my father delighted to mimic, showing him in the act of removing an imaginary pork loin from its hook, slapping it onto its wrapping paper, and then, so as to wet the paper—this was the fat of the jest—licking his fingers enthusiastically. . . . Surrounded by such uncouthness, it was good to have the recollection of the young Talmudist cherishing Torah in its integrity, continuing a tradition that went back through the ages to Sura and Pumbeditha and back farther still and farther to get lost in the zigzag and lightning of Sinai.

Curious to know what this paragon worthy of my emulation looked like, I asked my mother one day whether she had a photograph of Uncle Melech.

"A photograph!" My mother was shocked. "Don't you know that Jews don't make or permit themselves to be made into images? That's the second commandment. Uncle Melech wouldn't think of going to a photographer." I had to content myself, aided by my mother's sketchy generalities, with imagining Uncle Melech's appearance. Throughout the decades that followed, this afforded me an interesting pastime, for as the years went by and I myself changed from year to year, the image of Uncle Melech that I illegally carried in my mind also suffered its transformations.

When the first sign came that such a retouching of the photograph would soon be necessary, we did not know it for what it was. I was ten years old, it was the Feast of Rejoicing in the Law, and my father was at the synagogue when the letter from Uncle Melech was dropped through the slot over our threshold. My mother, who could not read—her respect for learning, I often thought later, stemmed largely from this fact—anxious to know who was speaking to her from afar, immediately dispatched me, with the letter, to my father. The synagogue was brightly illuminated throughout, even in those parts where no service was going on. On the tables reserved for study, there lay holy books, some of them still leafy with twigs of myrtle between the pages, last remnants of the Succoth ritual, serving now as bookmarks; but in the center of the synagogue, about the *almemar* and before the Ark of the Covenant, there was sound and exaltation. Wine had been drunk, and the Torah was being cherished with singing and dance.

As every year, the old Kuznetsov was already ecstatically exhilarated; his beard awry, his muddy features shiny pink, his very pockmarks hieratic like unleavened bread, he was dancing—a velvet-mantled scroll in his arms—with a fine other-worldly abandon, as his friends clapped hands in time. The cantor kept trilling forth pertinent versicles, answered by the congregation in antiphon. A year of the reading of the Law had been concluded, a year was beginning anew, the last verses of Deuteronomy joined the first of Genesis, the eternal circle continued. Circular, too, was the dance, a scriptural gaiety, with wine rejoicing the heart, and Torah exalting it to heights that strong wine could not reach.

My father, a copy of the Pentateuch before him, stood watching the sacred circle, smiling. Not a demonstrative man, he felt that joy had worthier means of expression than hopping feet; a shrewd man, too, he could not resist the reflection that most of those who were now jubilant with Torah either did not see Torah from year's end to year's end or, seeing, looked on it as knowingly as did the rooster on the page of the prayer of *Bnai Adam*. None the less, my father stood there smiling, smiling and happy, happy to see Torah honored even if only by hearsay.

I showed him the letter. "From Uncle Melech," he said, "that's a good letter for Simchas Torah." We withdrew to a more secluded spot in the synagogue. Looking up over his elbow as he read it, I saw that a number of words on the thin sheets were carefully, though not illegibly, blocked out, as if laid out in little coffins. I noted, too, that as my father read, from page to page his mood changed. The elation of a few minutes before left him. His nostrils widened and soon his lower lip was quivering. Tears slid down his face, to get caught, shining, in the hairs of his beard.

I looked up at my father, whom I had never seen weeping before, nor ever did again except for the time, two years before his passing, when on the High Holidays he joined in the prayer: *And in our old age cast us not aside, as our strength fails forsake us not. . . .*

"A pogrom," my father said quietly, "a pogrom in Ratno."

That night as from my bed I eavesdropped on the conversation of my father and mother, I learned the details of Uncle Melech's letter—of how the Balachovtzes, driving ahead of the fleeing Bolsheviks, had entered Ratno, and of how, summoning to their ranks the peasants of the region—yesterday's friends and neighbors—they had robbed and pillaged and murdered. The marked-out blocks on the letter, I gathered from the snatches of talk, from the choked sobbings that came in the dark of my room to my pillow, were the names of those who were no longer among the living: the old rabbi, Rabbi Heshel; Israel Meyer, the shochet, slaughtered with his own knife; our cousin Aryeh Leib, Yentel Baila's son; both daughters of Braina, the potter's daughter; and others, and others—names that I had heard often before, connected with some holy parable or comic anecdote, which now moved about my bedstead like ghosts.

There was also something else in that letter to which not much attention was paid that night: Uncle Melech's tone of bitterness. It was unmistakable. It is true that he quoted passages from the Bible enjoining resignation, but he also quoted Jeremiah: *Wherefore doth the way of the wicked prosper? Wherefore are all they happy that deal very treacherously?*

The letters from Uncle Melech that followed during the months thereafter contained no further reference to the massacre. Nor were they, as they had always been, any longer marked by witty allusion, or novel interpretation of Gemara, or parable and homily. Beginning with formal and flattering salutation, they reported that his health was good, inquired after ours, and in the more recent letters sought information about life in Canada. It was clear that something grave had taken place, not only in the four cubits of my uncle's ambience, but in his very soul. My father discussed with my mother sending him a ticket to come to Montreal. This was a sacrificing gesture, for my father's savings were meager, my mother feigned to propound all the arguments against such generosity, and finally my father sent a letter to Uncle Melech in which he made the suggestion that he would pay for his transportation and that he should leave forever the land of *Fonya Swine.*

To that letter there came no reply.

It was about a year later that there were brought to our house, on a Saturady night, two strangers, just arrived from Halifax, where they had debarked after their ocean voyage from Ratno via Liverpool. Their suits were cut different from ours. They wore caps. Their faces were lined and always held serious expressions except when they patted my head and I discovered that they had sunflower seeds in their pockets. They spoke with a great and bitter intensity.*

They had been in Ratno at the time of the pogrom. It was before the High Holidays, and everyone was waiting for the occasion to win from the

* Somehow my entire childhood is evoked through this incident. See *Gloss Aleph,* page 123.

Lord through prayer a happy and prosperous new year. Then they came—the drunken riffraff eager for sport, thirsty for blood. Those of the Jews who could fled, hiding from Ivan's wrath in cellars, in barns, in the forest, nostril-deep in water. But the old and the unimaginative, the helpless and the trusting, remained behind, and it was from among them that the victims were taken. "My own father was hanged before my eyes!" cried out the younger of the two strangers. "I know the men. I will yet return. Revenge!" He broke into an uncontrolled sobbing. It was contagious.

Murder by murder the pogrom was reconstituted for us by the passionate strangers. As my father inquired after relatives and old friends and as the strangers reported them well or among those perished for the Sanctification of the Name, it was a gruesome census that was being taken in my home. To make sure that the letters we had had from Uncle Melech were really his and not those of some good friend continuing the fiction of his life, to assure herself about her brother, from whom she had had no recent intelligence, my mother asked about Melech Davidson. "The *Ilui*? Didn't you hear?"

From the expression on my mother's face the stranger who spoke gathered that he was touching flesh. He hesitated, and then sought to change the subject.

"I'm his sister!" my mother importuned. "You've

got to tell me! What are you hiding? Woe is me!"
She knitted her fingers together and bent them backward. "Woe is me, and bitter! Him, too? But we got
letters from him!"

"No, no, not that at all. The *Ilui* is, thank God,
well. But he, too, received his portion of the calam-
ity. You can imagine what kind of bandits they were
who beset us. Your brother had the *chutzpa* to inter-
cede on behalf of the old rabbi, Rabbi Heshel; he
begged for his gray hairs, for his sanctity. 'Away,
dog!' the commander shouted at him. '*Pashol von!*
You're all Bolsheviks. All Jews are Bolsheviks!' When
the young Melech persisted in his plea, pointing out
that good Jews couldn't be Bolsheviks, that Bolshevism uprooted our religion, that Rabbi Heshel was
altogether a saint who didn't mix in worldly affairs,
Melech was taken out and publicly flogged for his
Jewish impertinence. He's recovered now. He was
ill for a while, but he's well now. In fact, two weeks
before we took the train from Ratno, he left the
town."

"And he wrote us nothing about it, my poor
brother! My fallen crown!"

At first we had only rumors of Uncle Melech's
destination. That he was playing with the idea of
leaving Ratno we knew from his inquiries about
Canada, but that he would finally choose as he did
came to my father like a thunderbolt.

Uncle Melech had joined the Bolsheviks! To

my father this was tantamount to apostasy. Here again I must rescue my father from the writings of his son; my father was no pharisee who stood shocked at a man's changing of his political convictions (they were not really political convictions that were involved, since Uncle Melech was always but an apolitical subject of the Czar). Nor was my father a man to be startled by rebellion; he had himself rebelled against the Romanovs—through flight. But Bolshevism—

Bolshevism meant the denial of the Name. My father's notions about the philosophy of Marxism were very primitive. Occasionally on Sundays, when there was a rotogravure section, he would buy the *Jewish Daily Forward* and read with an incredulous skepticism the theoretical articles which that journal featured. Invariably he would drop his paper with the helpless comment: "*Hegel-baigal!* The way these men do stir up a stew!" Considered from the point of view of common sense, the thing was simply ludicrous.

His antipathy to the dialectic, I am afraid, stemmed also from a nonintellectual source: his gratitude to the land of his adoption. This land hadn't given him much, mainly because he hadn't been a taker, but it had given him—this was no cliché to my father—freedom. Whenever one of his Ratno compatriots took it in his mind to run down Canada and its capitalismus, my father would withdraw a coin from his pocket and point to the image thereon engraved: "See this man, this is King George V. He looks like Czar Nicholas II. They are cousins. They wear the same beards. They have similar faces. But the one is to the other like day is to night. Nikolai might be a *kapora* for this one. After Nikolaichek you shouldn't even so much as whisper a complaint against this country!" This patriotism, it is to be admitted, was essentially pragmatic; it never did reach the fervor of his Canadian friend Cohen the cabinetmaker, the Cohen who had carved the ferocious lions guarding and upholding the Decalogue in front of the Ark of the Covenant in the *Chevra Thillim,* the martial Cohen who always bore on his person a Union Jack fringed with *tzitzith* and who threatened at the slightest provocation to fight the South African War over again; but it was nonetheless a loyalty solidly grounded, and one that was not likely to be impressed by a *pilpul* that drew all its examples, not from Canada, but from the Russia he had abandoned.

In that Russia, he agreed, it was high time that the Czar and his crew came to a black end. But Bolshevism—that had corollaries which were anathema. Soon malice began bringing my father the heinous details of Uncle Melech's conversion. Uncle Melech, it was reported, had shaved his beard. Uncle Melech, it was stated, was with the Russian cavalry; an imaginative gossip went so far as to add that Uncle

Melech had made his phylacteries part of his horse's harness. Uncle Melech, it was whispered, ate pork. He broke the Sabbath. He had become a commissar and was especially active with the zealots of the Society of Godlessness.

My mother would try to defend her brother's action—what he had lived through, she said, had upset his judgment—God spare us all such a testing! But it was an unconvinced defense and one that knew, even while it was being made, the arguments of its rebuttal. For it was clear that other people, too, had witnessed the pogrom and yet had not turned from their faith; many, moreover, had perished, while Uncle Melech had been saved; and even of the perished—what was man, to question the will of God?

We never again spoke of him in our house. But as the years passed I had no further need to rely upon my domestic sources for information; I could always pick up the latest news about him from the townsfolk of Ratno now resident in Montreal, whom I would meet at recurrent festivals and funerals. I was by this time attending the university and already had been conditioned to look at Marxism with a most unfilial impartiality, and so the reports of Uncle Melech's progress in the Communist Party not only failed to disturb me but indeed filled me with a secret pride. From these reports, received during the late twenties and early thirties, I made myself a new image of the uncle who together with angels had stood invisible and auspicious over my Hebrew lessons. It was a strange metamorphosis, this from Talmudic scholar, syllogizing the past, into Moscow student, conspiring a world's future. It is true that Uncle Melech never did rise to high office in the Communist bureaucracy—his clerical antecedents stood against him—but his talents, both linguistic and polemical, were immediately perceived and appreciated. He attended, during the late twenties, various schools in Moscow, and thence he blossomed forth as Comrade Krul, the international authority upon the decadence of European literature. Throughout these years we received of course no letters from him, and I heard of him and his exploits but twice: once when a dialectical essay of his appeared in English translation, and again when I read an account of the strike that he had organized among the employees of the Warsaw Bourse, where he had succeeded in keeping commodity transactions at a standstill for over a week.

It was the essay, however, that really interested me, for it constituted a remarkable instance of what happens when the Talmudic discipline is applied either to a belletristic or revolutionary praxis: Krul's quotations from European writing had the thoroughness, and in a sense the quality, of a concordance, and his argumentation was like nothing so much as like the subtilized airy transcendent *pilpul* of Talmud-commentary commentators. As for his matter, it was a series of curious alternations between prophetic thunder and finicky legalism; often he lapsed into parody, yet here and there one would be startled by either the justness of the irreplaceable word or the daring of the high imaginative flight.

The German invasion of Poland trapped him in Kamenets, not far from Ratno, where he was enveloped by the great smoke that for the next six years kept billowing over the Jews of Europe—their cloud by day, their pillar of fire by night.

EXODUS

WHEN as a young boy, the consolations and prophecies of Isaiah before me, I dreamed in the dingy Hebrew school the apocalyptic dream of a renewed Zion, always I imagined it as coming to pass thus: First I heard the roar and thunder of the battle of Gog and Magog; then, as silence fell, I saw through my mind's eye a great black aftermath cloud filling the heavens across the whole length of the humped horizon. The cloud then began to scatter, to be diminished, to subside, until revealed there shone the glory of a burnished dome—Hierosolyma the golden! Then lower it descended and lower, a mere breeze dispersed it, and clear was the horizon and before me there extended an undulating sunlit landscape.

My childhood vision, no doubt the result of a questionable amalgam between Hollywood and Holy Writ, was indeed fulfilled; but not in all its details and particularities. The cataclysmic war was there, the smoke, the thud and brunt of battle; but no golden dome. What was to be seen instead on the fifth day of Iyar was a forgathered company of men hitherto obscure, as anonymous as the *Bnai Brak,* who too had spent a night expatiating upon the miracles of exodus, met in surroundings not palatial, in a city which forty years earlier had had neither being nor name, to announce to the world on behalf of a people for whom they were as yet *noms de plume,* hardly *noms de guerre,* that henceforward in the domain of their forefathers they, nullifying all hiatus, intended to be, beneath the sovereignty of the All-Sovereign, sovereign.

My life was, and is, bound to the country of my father's choice, to Canada; but this intelligence, issuing, as it did, from that quarter of the globe which had ever been to me the holiest of the map's bleeding stigmata, the Palestine whose geography was as intimately known as the lines of the palm of my hand, filled me with pride, with exaltation, with an afflatus odorous of the royal breath of Solomon. I was like one that dreamed. I, surely, had not been of the captivity; but when the Lord turned again the captivity of Zion, I was like one that dreamed.

My dreaming was given a dream's authenticity when after the first year of the Stablishing my publisher invited me to undertake, for my spiritual advantage and his profit, a pilgrimage to Israel. It would be a good idea, he thought, if at this conjuncture in history I were to produce, after sojourning in the land, a volume of translations of the poems and songs of Israel's latest nest of singing birds. I was the only man, he flattered me, who could assume so difficult a task, I "whose translation from the Hebrew had ranged all the way"—he was already composing his blurb—"from the writings of the warbling *ibns* of the golden age of Spain to the pious stanzas of the convert Elisheva." Both his argument and his flattery were superfluous; on any excuse I was ready to make the journey.

Began, then, my hectic preparations, with visits to consulates, and cajolings of foreign-exchange bureaucrats, and submissions to the needles of doctors. One has to suffer to earn Jerusalem. Scarified I was, accordingly, against smallpox, punctured against typhus, pierced for tetanus, injected for typhoid, and needled with cholera; wounds and bruises were mine, and putrefying sores, which were not closed nor bound up nor mollified with ointment. The world, say the old liturgies, is full of "wild beasts that lie in wait"; these, my doctors thought, included not only the ravenous ones of the forest, the traveler's usual terror, but also the minute destroyers of the air: germs, viruses, microbes; against their encounter they pointillated upon my arms their prescribed prophylactic prayers.

My itinerary had already been arranged: I was to fly from New York, via Paris and Rome, to Lydda; and my passport had been duly visaed: it bore No. 9

of the records of the Israeli consul at Montreal—I was of the first *minyan*—when there arrived on my desk a fat heavily postmarked envelope. It had obviously been directed to my old address on the Avenue de l'Hôtel de Ville, whence we had removed not more than twenty years before, and was full of scrawled notations attesting to the blindman's buff that the post office had played before it had finally stumbled upon my actual whereabouts. Its return address was indicated as *Bari, Italia*, and its sender was Melech Davidson, not designated Signor—Uncle Melech.

It was like a voice from the beyond.* Eagerly I tore the envelope open and began reading the letter. I did not have to read very far to realize that this was not the Uncle Melech of my last imagining, the girded champion of the revolution. Even in its opening greetings, where I had expected to encounter the comradely salute, I noted the abandonment of the Marxist jargon. Instead Uncle Melech had reverted to the epistolary style of his Talmudic days and had addressed my mother, his sister, as "the virtuous woman prized above rubies," and my father as "the keen blade of jurisprudence, familiar of the Law, mighty hammer of Torah." The date he set down "with the help of God" as "the new moon of

---

* Premonition there had been, for it was shortly before the reception of this letter that I had composed my kinsmen's *Elegy*. See *Gloss Beth*, page 127.

Tammuz, five thousand seven hundred and nine, which in the reckoning of the ethnics is 1949."

There came back to me, as I read the letter, the recollection of my father's perusal of Uncle Melech's last communication, and I could not prevent the tearfulness that threatened to blur my vision. My father had passed on to his reward many years ago; my mother, lingering awhile—to gather up the things my father had forgotten?—followed some time thereafter; and this letter, intended for them, now came to me as last asset of my inheritance.

The Hebrew greeting ended, the letter continued in Yiddish:

"I pray your forgiveness for not having written to you all these years; nor will I enter now into explanations for my silence. It is too late for explanations." (Did Uncle Melech know?) "It is surely not because I haven't thought of you, it is because—let us say that it is because, having taken upon myself the yoke of exile, I deemed it also my duty that I should sunder myself from kith and kin. As if that were ever possible. . . . In the light of all that has happened, I know now that I was in error, in grievous error. Forgive.

"Today I write as one who having fled from out a burning building runs up and down the street to seek, to find, to embrace the kinsmen who were with him in that conflagration and were saved. And we were all in that burning world, even you who

23

were separated from it by the Atlantic—that futile bucket.

"I bless the Heavenly One for my rescue. It is wonderful to be alive again; to know that the trouble, the astonishment, the hissing is over; to eat, not husks or calories, but food; to have a name; and be of this world. Even now I do not know how it happened or by what merit it was I who was chosen, out of the thousands who perished, to escape all of the strange deaths that swallowed up a generation. At times I feel—so bewildered and burdened is my gratitude—that the numbered dead run through my veins their plasma, that I must live their unexpired six million circuits, and that my body must be the bed of each of their nightmares. Then, sensing their death wish bubbling the channels of my blood, then do I grow bitter at my false felicity—the spared one! —and would almost add to theirs my own wish for the centigrade furnace and the cyanide flood. Those, too, are the occasions when I believe myself a man suspect, when I quail before the eyes of my rescuers wondering *Why? Why did this one escape? What treaty did he strike with the murderers? Whose was the blood that was his ransom?* I try to answer these questions, but my very innocence stutters, and I end up exculpating myself into a kind of guilt.

"I try—I look about me at the Jews of this camp, the net of our accounting, and try to compose backwards from these human indices the book of our chronicles. I hear from the neighboring tent the voices of the castrati and evoke the images of the white-robed monsters who deprived them of race. I scan the tattooed arms—the man before me bears the number 12165—and wonder whether it is in gematria that there lies the secret of their engravure. I see them all about me, the men who cheated the chimney, those who by some divine antitoxin were preserved from the thirty-two fictitious diseases. Through the kindergartens of the orphans I proceed, and talk to children, and observe. I observe how it is that so many of them wear little lockets that break open, like cloven hearts, to reveal the picture of father or mother or brother lost, old-fashioned, poorly taken snapshots of the formal stance or the gay moment—they are everywhere—and I conceive the multitudinous portrait-gallery of our people: it hangs pendent from the throats of little children. Our small cenotaphs. And here in the secretariat of the camp I keep counting over and over again the puny alphabetical files to which we have been reduced. Yet from all of these studies and encounters I am not able to make me a chart of what actually happened; it is impossible. When the Lord turned again the captivity, I was like one that dreamed.

"All I can follow in clear sequence—and even here at the critical connectives it is only the hand of God that can explain—is what happened to me. It was late '39, and when the enemy swarmed over Poland, I found myself in Kamenets, still abashed by the treachery of the pact that the Soviets had made with the sons of Belial. In the midst of our anguish we were regaled with a dialectic which proved that fascism was but a matter of taste. The taste was bitter unto death. Almost I made my own the counsel of Rabbi Simon ben Yochai concerning those best of serpents who, too, ought to have their smooth skulls crushed. With a stroke of the pen, a dart of the tongue, they had handed over to perdition, those two-faced masters of thesis and antithesis, three and a half million souls. My ideology had been a saying of grace before poison.

"How it came to pass that during the more than four years that I had to remain in Kamenets I was not denounced as the Communist I no longer was—it would have been an ironical but just visitation—I shall not ever know. Perhaps it was because everybody was busy devising means for himself to remain obscure, unnoticed by the death's-heads who terrorized our streets, that no one thought of me; perhaps it was the loyalty of the valley of the shadow. There had been, indeed, occasions when the men with the eyes of ice had gone searching for their various categories of *Zigeuner* and *Bibelforscher*—I, in fact, could fall under both classifications—but the fact that I was now caftaned, bearded, and befringed apparently rendered me harmless. Is it not written that in the place where the repentant one stands, not even the complete saint may stand?

"These were years obsessed by a premonition of doom continually postponed. We were ghetto-ized, with none coming or going without special permission. We were catalogued: blue cards, yellow cards, red cards—our oppressors changed them at their whim so that even starvation in its various penultimate hues was uncertain. With the six-pointed Star of David we were inoculated against the world. We lived from prayer to prayer.

"Then one day—I remember it well, it was the Sabbath of the Bar Mitzvah of Rabbi Zelig's youngest son and came at the end of a long, shuddering week—the town was suddenly surrounded at all its exits. The commanding officer of Kamenets had been missing for over a fortnight, our oppressors had accused the Jews of having kidnapped or murdered him, and the ultimatum issued to the Town Council to produce him, if alive, within the week, had expired. In the public square the placards offering a reward for the discovering of the Commandant's body still glowered their gothic menace. In the meantime searches, which were but an excuse for brutality and pillage, were carried on in all houses.

"The Commandant was not found.

"It began in Rabbi Zelig's home, where a number of his relatives and some worthies of the community had gathered to congratulate the young boy who this day was being confirmed into the congregation of Israel. The boy, standing in front of Rabbi Zelig's Ark of the Covenant—public worship had been forbidden—was making his speech of self-dedication when there burst into the house a turmoil of heavy-booted soldiers. They were under the command of a young lieutenant who, it soon appeared, prided himself on being a specialist in Semitic affairs. . . . How shall I tell you, how shall I bring myself to write down, the abominations which took place that day! The Scroll of the Law was polluted: between its rods upon the parchment an infant was set and then tossed in the air—the specialist shouted: '*Hagba*'—was allowed to fall to the ground, its skull cracked crying: 'Father!' Our women were made to strip and circle the room—*hakofos,* explained the specialist—while the soldiery indulged in their obscene jests; and our men were each in turn called up to the improvised pulpit—*aliyoth,* said the authority—to receive their beard-pluckings and blows. Some—I among them—were allowed to go unscathed. It was these arbitrary exemptions, together with the guns which threatened immediate death, that induced and compelled the performance of the unspeakable ritual.

"The sport over, we were ordered out of the house, and outside observed that similar rituals were taking place in the other habitations of our ghetto. In the street there stood a truck with spades and mattocks; these were distributed to all the men. The specialist then addressed us. Information had come to the authorities, he said, that the body of the Commandant had been buried outside the town, near the abandoned mill. We were to dig that ground until we came upon it.

"Oh, that we had used our spades in a last battle for an honorable death!

"We dug that whole Sabbath afternoon. The suspected place, a considerable area, had been marked out, and after about three hours of digging —every stone we struck sent terror through our hearts—we stood in the midst of a great pit, deep and wide.

"The Commandant's body had not been found.

"It was as, at the order of the specialist, we climbed out of the pit that we realized that the revenge of our tormentors had not been staved off; for the whole horizon before us was dark with smoke, streamered here and there with tongues of flame. Fire had been set to the town. A great weeping arose among the women, crying: 'Our children! Our children!'

"We cursed in our hearts the man, whoever he was, who had laid hands upon the Commandant and made all of us the hostage of his luxury.

"Some rushed forward to go back into the burning town. It was as one of these was shot down that there screamed up the road which led to the mill a high-powered car, sounding its horn loudly. As it sped toward the field of the pit and skidded to a stop, there stood up in it, giving the outstretched salute, a tall, bemedaled, arrogant figure. The Commandant! He was alive! We had been saved!

" 'Praise be to the Lord!' cried Rabbi Zelig. 'He sleeps not, neither does He drowse, the Custodian of Israel!'

"Among the women ululations now alternated with crazy uncontrolled laughter.

" 'Silence!' The specialist was deeply conscious of his role. 'Do you not think that you Jews owe some celebration, some festivity, to the Commandant for his miraculous appearance?'

"The Commandant beamed.

" 'In front of the pit! Line up! Quick!'

"The order was obeyed.

" 'Now where are your musicians?'

"There stepped forward from the line our wedding company of four fiddlers, two flute-players, and the drummer.

" 'Give them'—the specialist turned to the soldiers in the truck—'give them their instruments.'

"And there they were, in the truck, the fiddles, the flutes, and the drum. All in readiness. The whole thing—disappearance and sudden miraculous appearance—all of it had been a prearranged plan. Terror gripped us. A wind passed over my face, as if a door of the world to come had been left ajar.

" 'And where is Itzka, your town idiot? He must lead the orchestra!'

"Itzka was pushed forward and a baton placed in his hand.

" 'Now, a *freilichs!*'

"Led with fantastic gestures by the flattered Itzka, the musicians trembled over their tune, at first hesitatingly, as if seeking and probing out their theme. Soon they reached the high ecstatic and repetitive notes, the expression of the bride's and bridegroom's ineffable union, the notes beyond which it was impossible to reach, so strange, so otherworldly—

" 'Fire!'

"The specialist's voice had barked; barked, too, the guns. The volley reached its marks: screams, *shma-Yisroels,* upflung arms, and great toppling into the pit.

"The Commandant beamed. The plan had worked according to schedule. The cunning Jews had been outwitted.

"The shooting continued for some time. Myself, I had been pushed at the first volley by a falling body onto one of the upper ledges of the pit, where I lay motionless. Two others fell upon me; their blood trickled on my skin. Now and again I heard the running agony of some who, holding their wounds, tried to flee; they were pursued and beaten to death. *One bullet to a man!* Rabbi Zelig's youngest son, the *bar mitzvah,* having been incompletely shot, crawled out of the grave. He was grabbed by one of the soldiers and flung back. *You are supposed to be dead, little Jew! Stay that way!* Soon the number of bodies heaped upon him stifled his cries.

"And all this time the musicians continued with the *freilichs,* which now and then trailed off into whinings, breaks, and falsettos. It was during one of these hesitations that the final volley was heard. The music was silenced; a last fiddle scraped.

"Darkness had fallen, and as I lay beneath my burden, my wrist under my mouth providing space for breathing, I could hear the soldiers pushing the pile of earth that had been dug up during the day back into the pit. The soldiers were exhausted, and contented themselves with simply a general covering layer of earth.

"The grave groaned.

"A soldier slapped with the back of his spade upon the place that had groaned. 'We'll finish it tomorrow,' he said, 'the Jews are bedded for the night.'

"As their footsteps died away, I heard one of them shouting, as if he had turned back: 'You may go now, Itzka. Kamenets is yours.'

"It was the middle of the night when I rose from the grave. All was now silence; the groans had ceased; the earth trembled no more. I rose up and, a shadow of the shadows of the night, I made my way toward the neighboring forest.

"There will be, I hope, other occasions when I may write you of the times that went over me, of the kindness of the wild beasts of the wood who did *not* seek my life, of the ruses and deceptions I used to disguise myself, and of that good peasant family over whose house there presided the image of the man of Galilee, who hid me and fed me and preserved me. Of them, and of how they kept alive in me the human mind so that I did not collapse to walk on all fours, I shall at another time attest. Now I hasten toward my future.

"When the end came, when the highways of Europe were at last cleared of the cogged armored monsters, I came out of my concealment and joined in camp after camp the remnants of our people. And now I am at Bari; I am promised that soon I shall be able to board ship for Haifa.

"Already there come to this harbor the rescuing ships of the Israeli navy. I stand here on the shore and watch them as they take on their passengers. Clarion names they bear, these ships: *Negba*—to the south! *Kedma*—to the east! *Atzmaouth*—independence! I stand on the shore here watching them, it is my one engrossing vision. Before me there extend the waters of the Mediterranean—blue; and its foam—white: an Israeli flag. Above me there stretches the Mediterranean sky—blue; and its clouds—white: an Israeli banner. And between flag and banner and banner and flag there proceed these the pauperized rich argosies of our future. Oh, let the nations of the world keep their mighty armadas, their hosts of dreadnoughts, their potent fleets sweeping the waters of the deep! Theirs be the leviathans of steel and plate; the proud galleons, the sweated galleys—theirs! Ours, these overhauled corvettes, these leaking tubs, these discarded bottoms all of steerage compact—no flotilla in the world can rival them, no navy compare! For they carry a cargo unknown to the annals of the sea—a cargo of re-membered bones—and to the last landfall they make their way—a Navy of Redemption!

"I long to board one of these ships. But I must wait my turn. In the meantime I pause over my hope, I revolve it—as ben Bag-Bag was wont to do to the texts of Holy Writ—about and about. I weigh it, savor it, seek in all its aspects to realize and absorb. I make an introspective game out of it, a sacred play, as if with palm leaf shaken to the four winds, as if with citron held and palmed and blessed.

"A game; I say it to myself in language Biblic:

And it came to pass that the word was spoken unto Melech ben David, saying: Get thee out of thy country, and from thy

kindred, and from thy father's house. And
go thee forth to thy kinsmen and thy kins=
men's country, to the house of thy father's
father, which in these latter days has been
builded and set up again. And I will shew
thee a land . . .

"Or I read to myself a Mishna:

On the day of the redemption and at the
time of the rebuilding of Erez Israel,
what shall be the benediction to be uttered?
The benediction of shehichianu. Rab says:
The benediction prescribed to be said on
the appearing of a monarch, or wise man.
Others say: The benediction of the Tish=
bite.

"And I make Talmudic commentary:

The benediction of the Tishbite—what is
it? It is a benediction not yet composed,
the Tishbite Elijah will compose it. Said
the learned men of Babylon: Israel not yet
reconstructed—how then is one to know
the form prescribed for such occasion. Let
the time come, and the heart talk.

"Or I let my soul gambol among the cumuli of
Cabbala:

When the years were ripened, and the
years fulfilled, then was there fashioned

Aught from Naught. Out of the furnace there issued smoke, out of the smoke a people descended. The desert swirled, the capitals hissed: Sambation raged, but Sambation was crossed. . . ."

LEVITICUS

S the plane roared over the Atlantic, and I read and re-read my uncle's letter, his enthusiasm took hold of me and I saw myself, too, as part of the great re-enactment, knew myself borne to my destination, if only for a spying out of the land, "on the wings of eagles." My very levitation seemed a miracle in harmony with the wonder of my time; through my mind there ran the High Holiday praise of God for that He did "suspend worlds on withoutwhat," even as my plane was suspended, even as over the abyss of recent history there had risen the new bright shining microcosm of Israel.

There grew in me also a deflecting compulsion to go visit my uncle at Bari. My mother, I knew, would have wanted me to do this; my father, vindicated and reconciled, would have rejoiced; and I, now of a diminished tribe, felt that I could not forgo even an uncle never seen or known. Moreover, the distance between incognito uncle and nephew unmet had, during these years, disappeared; the disparity in age—he was but fifteen years my senior—had now but little significance. It occurred to me, above all, that Uncle Melech might be in need and I might be of help. I more than owed it to him. Was he not, in a sense, responsible for my pilgrimage? Had it not been his name that had encouraged me forward from the first twisted aleph of my schoolbook to the latest neologisms of Hebrew poetry? I made arrangements in Paris, therefore, to terminate my plane flight at Rome, whence I would proceed to Bari.

I had never been to Rome before; I would have liked to linger awhile in this renowned city, to visit the ghetto where the wonderful Immanuel, Dante's friend, first weaver of the Hebrew sonnet, had written his re-echoing *Tophet and Eden.* But Bari, I felt, could not attend delay.

The delay would not have mattered. Arrived at the camp, I found that Uncle Melech was no longer there. He and a Nachum Krongold had left six weeks before for Rome.

The camp-manager, a methodical and efficient man, but not immune, apparently, to the wiles of gossip, volunteered the story. He didn't know Davidson's address in Rome, but Monsignor Piersanti, he thought, could direct me to him. He used the word *Monsignor* as if it were an injector, and waited for symptoms to show on my face. I have no doubt they did, for he continued to tell me that the Monsignor was a very fine priest, full of understanding and sympathy, who used to visit the camp often, at which time it was Davidson who would conduct him around. The camp-manager feared, however, that the Monsignor was somewhat of a fisher of men. In troubled waters, he said, was good fishing. Today, in the light of what had transpired, he was really at a loss to say who had guided whom, Davidson the Monsignor or the Monsignor Davidson.

I could feel the blood rushing to my face. I wanted the man to say it, explicitly.

"You no doubt know," he parabled, "of the four men who would gaze into paradise: Ben-Azzai, Ben-Zoma, Rabbi Akiva, and That Other. Ben-Azzai gazed, and died. Ben-Zoma gazed, and went mad. Rabbi Akiva cried out: 'When you arrive at the stones of polished marble pure, do not exclaim: *Water, water!*' And That Other cut down the plant."

Uncle Melech, then, a cutter-down of plants, an uprooter, a convert! It shocked the thirty score inhibitions of my upbringing. My father had been right after all. Unstable as water, fickle as wind, That Other!

I remembered again Uncle Melech's letter and that troubling parenthesis about the good peasant family who had saved him. Gratitude, its tortuous inscrutable wild twistings! Now I certainly had to find him, for his sake and for our name's sake.

The Monsignor, I was told, could be found at the Library of the Vatican. Monsignor Piersanti was, as the camp-manager had described him, a man full of sympathy and understanding. He had, too, a very courtly manner, was extremely well read—I got the impression that it was his special duty to read all the books on the Index—and time passed quickly in his company. He seemed, above all, to be a student of the maladies of the age. As we talked of the atrocities that had made lurid our decade and of the unplumbable depths from which their motives sprang, the Monsignor was double-edged with paradox aimed at the easy explanations that both the economists and the psychiatrists had to offer for the world's ills. It was as if he were plucking playfully a tuft of Marx's beard, a tuft of Freud's; not bitter, he was most engaging; and then, speaking more seriously, he maintained that the plague was much more deeply rooted than that, the real cause was the ubiquitous festering immanence of Sin. A diagnostician of the soul, he gave me the feeling at times that he was looking at mine, palpating it, percussing it.

I brought the conversation back to my original inquiry. Yes, he knew Melech Davidson very well. He was my uncle? Really? A fine spirit, but somewhat uncertain. A great battle was being fought in my uncle's soul; sometimes he, the Monsignor, thought that the Light was beginning to break, but often, much too often, my uncle seemed to fall back into the darkness. He understood very well that it wasn't an easy thing for a man brought up in one belief suddenly to come to an awareness that another was the true one; in His own time Christ had to suffer on the tree before even the apostles learned steadfastness; the road to Damascus, though full of vision, was also full of peril and pitfall.

Then Uncle Melech had not yet gone over? He had not been baptized? No; Uncle Melech, he regretted to say, was a man of many relapses and backslidings. But he was climbing ever upward. It was true that he hadn't heard from him for some time, but he felt certain that Uncle Melech was wrestling valiantly with his doubts, and that in the end he would find the way. His way would have to be different from that of others his presented a difficult case: his early fervor, his atheist delirium, his spiritual vacillations, all of these showed that essentially Davidson's was a religious soul; he had the vocation, he heard the Voice, but he could not, blinded and deafened as he had been by his own tragic experience, tell the direction from which it came.

"To everyone his path. I tried to engage your uncle on the right one by leading him from the things that he appreciated first to those which he only mildly appreciated and then to those which he as yet did not appreciate at all. Your uncle, as you may know, has a not inconsiderable understanding of what among the forms is beautiful and correct. He derives it, moreover, not only from emotional but from cerebral sources; it is the appetency of his faith seeking reason and order. In my long conversations with him concerning European literature, I soon discovered that in his categorizing of the enduring and the ephemeral your uncle, though he lingered sensuously over the externals of expression, at length invariably directed himself to the core of ethical content. He greatly loves the right word, but he loves righteousness more. This, to me, was an inviting beginning: it showed that Davidson had an instinctive feeling for morality."

"Original virtue?"

"Not altogether. You forget his hesitations, his going two paces forward, one pace back. That's progress, of course, but it makes a very jagged spiritual graph. It took me, for example, some time before I succeeded in persuading him to visit the Sistine Chapel—have you been there yet? He had the old bias against images and, I suppose, against entering our places of worship. At the same time he wished ardently to see Michelangelo's paintings, he remembered so admiringly illustrations of them that he had seen in books. I, for my part, and, believe me, for his, desired very much that he see these masterpieces of Catholic art, for I hoped that, like the painter, he would be led from the Old Testament scenes to the New Testament truths. Michelangelo's sense of order, I felt, and, above all, his sublimity would appeal to him."

The Monsignor paused, meditative.

"He didn't go?" I asked.

"He went—but he did not come back. Instead he wrote me, in Hebrew—fortunately I read Hebrew, it is an aid to the comprehension of the Scriptures—and there, in his letter, was the old Adam again. Please do not misinterpret the epithet. I understood fully, painfully, the agony from which this letter was written. But I perceived also its vanity, its attempt, in the midst of self-pity, to imitate Michelangelo. Davidson had missed the point. It was another Imitation I had had in mind. Do you read Hebrew? Good." He rummaged among some papers on his desk. "I must have it here. Yes, here it is. The first page is missing."

He held up the pages, sorrowfully.

"Would you care to read it? Unfortunately, I have another appointment now, so take it with you. Perhaps when you bring it back we shall have a conversation about it."

The audience was at an end. I thanked the Monsignor for his kindness. I deeply appreciated the interest he had taken in my uncle, I regretted only that now I had no address to go to in search of my kinsman. The Monsignor sympathized; he had faith, however, that eventually my uncle would let us have intelligence of him; there would be a showing forth, an epiphany. He smiled.

It was with mixed feelings and harried by many insistent questions that I left the presence of the Monsignor. Why was the first page of the letter missing? Was it because it had included my uncle's address? Why was the Monsignor so sure that my uncle would be found? Had Uncle Melech indeed taken the unthinkable step? Was he keeping himself concealed until with proper éclat his conversion could be announced to the world? I recalled with fear and misgiving the affair of the chief rabbi of this very city, the apostate Zolli, who but a year ago had consternated his congregation with just such a timed and scheduled betrayal.

I was consumed with an eagerness to read the letter, now safe but obsessive in my pocket. At the same time I was afraid to read it, lest its contents corroborate my suspicion. Would the Monsignor so readily have confided to me his personal mail if it had not contained the dreaded revelation? Wasn't he really trying to soften a blow by postponing its delivery, by affording me the protection of private reading?

As I walked out into the bright classic day I must have presented an erratic spectacle to the passing Romans—a man walking a block, stopping, withdrawing from his bosom pocket a letter, unfolding it, reading it for a space, folding it, putting it back, and walking on. It was a difficult mode of reading; it bewildered me. I failed to excerpt at random, as I had thought I might, the answer to the query that was troubling me. The letter had to be read, I saw, slowly, consecutively. I looked for some place where I could sit down and at my leisure peruse my uncle's epistle to the Romans.

At length I found myself a bench before one of those many sculptured fountains which add to the beauty and music of Rome. I did not proceed, however, immediately to read the letter; I was tired, I wanted to rest a bit before facing all that it might contain. In my mind I was almost convinced that my uncle had severed himself from the congregation of Israel—so much so, in fact, that under the incantation of the fountain, bubbling and scattering before me in a continually transparent meditation, I got lost in a sequence of thought which, beginning by assuming Uncle Melech a Christian, soon saw him ordained a priest, elevated a bishop, chosen a cardinal, and finally elected a pope. There had been a Jewish pope—Anacletus?—once before, had there not? A second was not impossible. Besides, if the Principal could be a Jew, why not His vicar? The notion must have pleased me—our perverse family pride!—for when I suddenly became conscious of whither my meandering reverie had led me, I did not turn back in horror, but on the contrary toyed with the imagined situation's fascinating possibilities.

I saw then His Holiness Melech I seated on the papal throne, his Jewish origin ever a potent though secret impulse within him. I saw him as he performed the annual cycle of religious rite, and saw him as, lord of all realms spiritual, he brought his sanction and influence to bear upon temporal affairs. I saw, too, the long round of his encyclicals, their initial phrases flashing rubric fire, until at last the *Nunc dimittis* issued—the pronouncement the world had so long awaited. It was indeed worthy of His Holiness, and now with the full flawless power of his infallibility Uncle Melech proclaimed it to mankind: the abolition of all creeds, save Faith's supernal behest; the amalgamation of religions: Christianity, Judaism, Mohammedanism, a trinity made one. As the Latin periods of the encyclical rolled through my imagination, the world seemed to be fashioned anew again, while its labor, like the labor of the first creation, came to rest in the universe's harmony, sabbatical in universal peace.

"Bomba atomica! Amer-icano!"

The exclamation shattered my dream, and then in coalescing fragments shot me back onto the hard real bench, in the fountained park, amidst a group of smiling Italians. One of them I recognized.

I had made Settano's acquaintance the evening

before in the hotel bar, where he had impressed me as a much-traveled man, familiar of Europe's metropolitan slums, a disliker of Truman, and, as he himself phrased it, a polylingual autodidact. When after several Scotch and sodas I had ordered—out of pure thirst and nostalgia—a Coke (this beverage was just beginning its competition with the true Falernian), he had scoffed at me, styled me a typical emissary of the new religion, a sound, orthodox Cocacalian. I had spitefully accepted the compliment and—*pour l'épater*—had expatiated upon the beauty of the Coca-Cola bottle, curved and dusky like some Gauguin painting of a South Sea maiden, upon the purity of its contents, its ubiquity in space, its symbolic evocations—a little torchless Statue of Liberty. I had wantonly poetized thereon, rhapsodized; and the more lyrical I became, the greater grew his annoyance.

But really angry he never became. What he desired, I soon perceived, was to provoke *me* to anger and indiscretion, although about what I did not as yet know. I refused, however, to get drawn into a discussion of the relative merits of East and West, and every time he dwelt on the superiority of his favored longitudes, I shifted to the latitudes, praising Italy as a flagon of the warm south, praising Canada as the true north, strong and free, praising, praising, approving everywhere God's apolitical zones of temperature. Settano, for his part, shifted his ground—it was no longer points of the horizon we were talking about, but philosophies—and dogmatically asserted his materialist interpretation of history; there was no other, he was very simple who thought otherwise. I recognized in his challenging insistence an attempt to push me into a position where I would be advancing America as an example of spirituality. The decoy was too obvious and I ignored it. Instead, I brashly advanced *myself* as an example of spirituality—heckled only by the hybris of the Coca-Cola belch—and damned all materialisms, hailed the mystic, praised only the transcendental.

There were moments in the course of our conversation when he looked at me as if I were pitiably naïf, and other moments when he narrowed his eyes in an unconcealed effort to pierce through the guise of my dissembling. It was quite clear to me that he thought that I was some sort of agent. I felt picaresquely flattered and, for his thinking so, set him down as a spy and agent himself.

The evening's game had amused me immensely. After all, I was looking for neither Operation X nor Plan D, but only for my mother's brother—and the evening had ended with a quasi-friendship, both of us at last quaffing it down with Canadian V.O. As an abbreviation, he said, for vodka. He then bade me good-night, *Americano.*

"I am not an American. I'm a Canadian."

"Is there a difference? Isn't Canada the forty-ninth state?"

"On the contrary. The States are our eleventh province!"

His laughter—the gall of the Canuck! the utter absurdity!—rang through the corridor.

And now, as if to quasify our friendship further, here he was again, smiling that dialectical smile of his. Had one of those comrades of his followed me? Had I been seen issuing from my audience? Now surely must Settano have convinced himself that I was weaving some dark clerical design to be stained, in due course, with tincture of cola.

I was, I must confess, a little afraid. It was true that I was completely surrounded by smiles, like crescent satellites; none the less I felt singularly uncomfortable beneath all this blandness. Nor was my discomfort eased when, amiably grinning, Settano put his question:

"And how is His Holiness today?"

For a short crazy moment I suspected him of having read my thoughts. How otherwise did he know that he had just interrupted the final encyclical of Pope Melech I? This was ridiculous. I had been followed and the greeting referred to my interview.

"I trust he is well," I replied. "I did not see him. . . . And how's Joe?"

"Then what did you go there for? Absolution?"

He put the question as if it were but bantering small talk, in tone so couched and with gesture so introduced that had I resented it, my resentment would have looked surly, barbarian. I didn't care any longer for our ambiguous play, it was getting tiresome; so I told him in short, insultingly simple sentences—that ends the matter, doesn't it?—of my quest for my uncle.

Obviously he did not believe me. "If I knew," he said, "how to decode the name Uncle Melech, your story would perhaps be informative. As it is, I am beginning to believe that the revolution is really round the corner. . . . When a Jew goes to the Monsignor!"

Pleased, he turned to translate his wit to his companions. They found it uproariously funny. With many Italian gestures in which the open palm and fluttering fingers and weaving arm announced their mock credulity, they repeated the phrase one to another; then, as if in concert, they fell silent, and menacing.

The fountain continued its brilliant introspection.

Settano broke the silence. "Let's go," he said, "for a walk."

"I'm tired. It's nice here."

"*Andiamo!*"

His friends, a council of menace about me, looked as if they hoped I would refuse.

I rose from the bench.

The dialogue was getting much too melodramatic for my taste. I had intended, that happy day when I had risen from La Guardia Field, a voyage in search of the jewels of Hebrew poesy, not this forced Roman march. I didn't like it at all. I tried, therefore, at this point to recapture our original tone of banter, to bring back the pseudo-playfulness of our first salutation, and inquired—it must have been pathetic—with a false histrionic bravado: "Whither, O Romans?"

"I want to help you," Settano said. "I want to help you find your uncle. But where? Well, let me see. A man of no great means in a big city, where is he likely to be found? Where? Ah, I have it. He will be found, if transient, in its brothels; if resident, in its black market. . . . Where would you prefer, signor, to begin your search?"

I scorned to answer. Uncle Melech in a brothel! Uncle Melech a black-marketeer!

The fury of my silence set him laughing again.

"You are, I see, definitely not a realist. Well, then, how about you yourself, in your quality of tourist? Wouldn't you like to see the sights—the oldest profession and the newest?"

"I think I will watch the fountain."

I returned to the bench, stretched out my legs, and gave myself to the watching of the fountain. Settano sat down beside me and put his right hand in his coat pocket. "Isn't it beautiful?" he said.

Suddenly I felt the hard shrouded nozzle pressing against my thigh. Charmingly Settano looked into my face. "We will walk?" he said. "*Si?*"

"*Si.*"

Now, standing up and surrounded by my friend's friends—two in front and two following—I was really scared. As we walked in silence, Settano and I, the Italian made casual conversation. To anyone who looked closely, however, the formality of escort was inescapable.

But nobody looked closely. The citizens of Rome were intent upon their own business, and five men marching together along a main thoroughfare, even though one of them wore a gay tie and diamond-checked socks, was nothing to stop at.

We continued thus in phalanx for several blocks, when, strolling toward us, I noticed two *carabinieri.* The police of Rome are tall and they always come in pairs. But Settano caught my look and read my thought. "Here," he said, "look in this shop window! And one word from you, and you'll get it in the heart!"

We all looked in the shop window. On display were vases, chinaware, cutlery, trays. Where I stood I faced a large empty silver platter. The window, it appeared, was somewhat dusty and brought back to us our own reflection. It was with a great unease that I observed that my own head, level with the tray, seemed to be mirrored as lying upon it.

The *carabinieri* passed.

We left the shop window and turned onto a side street that was comparatively deserted. Here again we continued for several blocks. The Italians had ceased talking to one another; all of us walked on in silence. My fear was increasing from step to step. I was desperate.

"Tell me, Settano"—I had stopped in my tracks —"in what capacity are you leading me now, as black-market commission agent or as pimp?"

"Get in that doorway!" he said, waving me to it with his coat-flap. I obeyed.

"Search him!"

I was helpless. Yet, as two of the Italians went through my pockets, I felt grateful that all that I was suffering was a search; my rash terror-prompted question might easily have led to worse. There were handed to Settano my passport, my billfold, my key-ring, my small change, and Uncle Melech's letter.

"We don't want your filthy money, nor your papal keys," he said, returning the articles to me. "Nor your passport—*cittadino canadese*. But this" —he waved it before my eyes—"the Monsignor's letter, this we must have!"

"But it's my uncle's! It's of no interest to you! I haven't even read it yet. You're making—"

"If we're making a mistake, you'll get it back. And now, if you will excuse us, you can walk by yourself to the main street. And don't look back!" The coat-flap was active again.

When I got out of what I safely estimated to be Settano's range, I did look back. But the street was deserted.

On the main street I hailed a taxi and drove to the hotel.

I felt very depressed. I kept reproaching myself that I should not have allowed the robbery to take place without outcry. To have come so near to having word from Uncle Melech, and then to have his word snatched from me! It was humiliating. Humiliating also would be my visit to the Monsignor to tell him what had happened and to ask again for a résumé of Uncle Melech's letter. What a way to begin my trip! What a story to forget about!

I thought of going to the police, but dismissed the idea as totally unpractical. What would I tell them—that somebody had filched a letter of mine? Surely more serious crime was keeping them busy these days. And for one who wanted to get out of Rome as soon as possible, a police complaint, with its inevitable delays and adjournments, was hardly an expedient toward haste. I went to a movie instead.

It was a wise decision. The movie was *Shoe Shine,* a piece of prolonged and unrelieved tragedy that, though communicated with the casualness of reportage, brought to the spectator a more than dantesque catharsis, for this inferno was filled with children. In different circumstances the picture would have made muggy the climate of my heart, inducing, as had happened before, a continuing but unidentified melancholy, a sadness that refused to give its name. As it was, it served only to alleviate my chagrin; the world was full of misfortune greater than mine; I was a sybarite even to wince at my loss.

But when I returned to my room that night—there it was, Uncle Melech's letter, blank blue-lined envelope and all, slipped under my door!

Eagerly I read it, and with increasing relief and pleasure. How welcome, how hallelujah-sweet were these lines written on first seeing the ceiling of the Sistine Chapel! * He had not been quite precise, the Monsignor, in describing the language in which it was couched as Hebrew; Hebrew it largely was, but dominated by a polyphonous evocation of Aramaic—the parle of Pumbeditha, Sura's cryptic speech! It would be, I decided after my emotional gratification had given way to literary appraisal, the first of the translations of my anthology. The singing bird, it was true, was not yet of the land, but

* Its full text is given in *Gloss Gimel,* page 135.

there could be no doubt of his direction. He was definitely southing; other parts of his letter might be ambiguous, but that was orient clear.

For the letter was really a sort of homily touching Michelangelo's intuitions and intentions, a sermon about the nature of man. It strove to show that although Buonarotti intended only to depict scenes of the first chapter of Genesis, what he had actually done was to signalize the various dilemmas of the human plight. Uncle Melech dwelt with admiration upon the figures of the twenty athletes whose stance and gestures proclaimed everywhere the vividness with which they remembered God's first fingertouch; he indulged also in a little excursus about the smaller supporting figures to whom was vouchsafed a less spiritual mnemonic of that great experience; and out of these descriptions he sought to establish his basic premise: the divinity of humanity.

And it is at this point that Uncle Melech, standing beneath the figure of Ezekiel, is struck by the contrast between this lofty concept and the events of recent history. Making reference, to show the direction of his thinking, to the Sistine lime pit of his own day, he proceeds, with midrashic ingenuity, to characterize each of the nine mighty panels. He does not overlook, of course, the medallions, which tell, every one, a tale of violence and bloodshed. The scene depicting the drunkenness of Noah he takes as a parable of murder, which is an intoxication with blood; *The Flood* he considers a general allusion to his own time; in *Noah's Sacrifice* he discovers a veiled illustration of the slaughter of his generation's innocents; and *The Expulsion from Eden* he ingeniously regards as having proleptic reference to the world's refugees, set in flight, not by an angel, but by a double-headed serpent.

But it is with *The Creation of Adam and of Eve* that his indictment begins to become explicit and is particularized. His syllogisms, though very simple, are dreadful in their conclusions. Since Adam is created in the image of God, the killing of man is deicide! Since Eve is a reproductive creature, the murder of the mortal is a murder of the immortal! Heinous crimes—it is at the threshold of his non-Jewish contemporaries that he lays them, corpse upon accusing corpse.

Uncle Melech had made his point. The Monsignor, surely, had not expected such comment concerning the manner in which Christian history had interpreted Christian art. (Nowhere in his letter did Uncle Melech advert to the scenes from the life of Christ that Michelangelo had painted, as if *sub rosa,* about the larger outlines of his, work.) Uncle Melech had made his point; and I had my answer.

But there was more. Uncle Melech was not content with deducing from the frescoes their prophecies of doom and slaughter; triumphantly he deduced from them also the sure promise of survival. The seven colors that Michelangelo had used are to him a rainbow pledging cessation of flood. His people might be maimed but, as a people, could not be destroyed. *The Creation of the Sun and Moon* he therefore reads as a foretelling of survival; the planets spring back into place for those for whom the heavens had been darkened. But *The Separation of Light from Darkness* provides him his climactic opportunity. Here, where Michelangelo for the first and only time dared to show (and not show) *the face of God*, here Uncle Melech chose as the place finally to assert his adherence to the creed. In a single circular sentence, without beginning or end, he described God coming to the rescue of His chosen. It was a sentence in which I distinguished, between commas, in parentheses, and in outspoken statement, all of the thirteen credos of Maimonides.

Uncle Melech had underlined his answer to the Monsignor.

I folded the letter and put it back into its envelope. The day had ended brighter than it had begun. Uncle Melech was hidden, but not lost.

Among the letters of introduction that solicited on my behalf the courtesy of all whom it might so please, there was one addressed to the officials of the American Joint Distribution Committee at Via de San Basilio 9. They, if anyone, would know, I thought, whether Uncle Melech was still at Rome; and when, on the following morning, I repaired to this place, I felt, even as I entered its vestibule, that here there was good possibility of succeeding in my search.

For here, waiting on the various landings and in the antechambers of this building, which housed also consulates and international societies, were numerous groups of jargoning Jews engaged in conversations loud, gesticulative, or whispered. The groups overflowed also into the street, and there, in front of the little restaurants displaying in their windows straw-girt wine-bottles and basketed bread, broke up into dialogues, triumvirates, family scenes. As I made my way up the stairs—the elevator was out of order—snatches of their talk reached me to make in my mind a polyglot echoing of the more palpable anxieties of the exodus.

"*Der yid beim tzvaten tisch iz zeir a simpatisher. . . . Treren. . . .*"

"*Mais oui, on parle français à Quebec.*"

"*In Detroit ich habe eine uncle gefunden.*"

"*Derveil macht er a leben mit di Amerikanski dollaren. . . . Fleishige un milchige.*"

"*Az Amerikai di vat magazin nagya jo izlesu.*"

"*Basta!*"

"*Un restaurant mic, si se poate un bar de coctail.*"

"Yehudai hagalut, dorshai hagalut . . . zocharnu et habtzolim v'et hashomim."

Whoever of European Jewry was not waiting in a camp was attending, it seemed, in person or by proxy, outside the door of some JDC office. Someone here would surely know of Uncle Melech. Pushing through the conclave of geographers and diplomats—it elated me to be part of this resilient crowd, planning, pleading, queuing, and heading itself into its variegated future—I presented my letter at the information desk and was soon ushered into the presence of the director. I explained the purpose of my visit. "Ah, Davidson," he said, "Krongold will tell you all about him. The third door to the left. Just knock and walk in."

He lifted the receiver of his phone and, as I shut the door, I could hear him announcing my coming to Krongold.

Tall, red-headed, freckled, rustic, the man who rose from behind the desk of the third door to the left extended his hand and said: "A friend of Davidson's?"

"A nephew."

"A nephew! Did you know him at all?"

"Only by hearsay and blood-ties."

Krongold made himself comfortable behind his desk.

"A unique character. Nobody like him. You

never could tell one minute what he was going to do next."

"What is he doing now?"

"God knows. He's supposed to be looking after future immigrants to Israel. But whether he's doing his job or implementing some design of his own, I wouldn't undertake to say. Your uncle, whom, believe me, I know well—we were at Bari together, we came to Rome together, and after a while could even through silence carry on our conversations—your uncle has one great passion: ideas. In his life they substitute for the woman he never married. But unfortunately he is not, in ideas, a monogamist. An idea passes before him, it finds favor in his eyes, he courts it: it is love. Finally he embraces it, the idea turns to honeymoon ideal, soon acquires domesticity, it is a wife of an idea, and then—a new one passes by, walking and mincing as it goes, making a tinkling with the feet—and Davidson casts his eyes after that. There was a Monsignor—"

"I know the story, I know it. But that's over, isn't it?"

"Forgive me. I didn't mean—I knew all along that the flirtation wouldn't last. Davidson is, it is true, a philanderer of ideas, but to the basic one he remains faithful: loyalty. He'd never leave a besieged city, a wounded companion. Under no circumstances would he go over to a majority. In fact, the idea most appealing to him is—to join the minority. In the pattern of his life that is to be seen everywhere. And it is this pattern that brought about the break between us."

—?

"A philosophic one. Davidson has not yet got the *galuth* out of his system. He hates it, he loves it. He is infatuated with suffering. And I, I am sick of martyrdom, sick of the passive role, sick of the equation *I suffer; therefore I exist*. Both of us were working here at Rome, both of us committed to going to Israel; but somehow delays were always taking place, once for so-called technical reasons and another time through our own fault; in the meantime, here we were still stranded.

"Then one day I said to him: 'Let's leave. The JDC will arrange it, let's get on the next boat.' Frankly, at that time I not only wanted to put an end to the cul-de-sac, this *Nachtasyl* of our life; I wanted also to get Davidson out of Rome, away from his religious explorations, his visits to the Vatican. I know now that I need not have worried about this, but I didn't want to take any chances. So I put it to him, the last change of scene, the final change of heart. Do you know what he answered? He wasn't ready."

"But I have a letter of his which is very eloquent of his impatience to reach Israel."

"He had a change of heart. He would leave Rome, but not for Haifa. And here it was that he showed that he was not yet fully rid of the Diaspora infection. He desired to go to Casablanca."

He waited to see the effect of his revelation. By this time, however, nothing that Uncle Melech would do would have surprised me. If he had said: "to the planet Saturn," I should also have waited for particulars.

"He wanted to feel in his own person and upon his own neck the full weight of the yoke of exile. He wanted, he said, to be with his Sephardic brothers, the lost half of Jewry. So there it was again, that passion for belonging to the minority. Let it not offend you, but I pitied him, pitied him for these sentiments, this nostalgia for suffering, this wallowing; but what could I do? I wanted to get him away from Rome. So I spoke to the chief, told him what a learned man your uncle was, what a fine administrator, how well he would understand the problems of the Moroccan Jews, with whom we were so concerned, and obtained him a job at Casablanca. I hope he has not got hold of the Koran."

I was thankful for the little joke.

Two days later, after having got my passport properly visaed for entry into the Sultanate of Morocco, I was on the plane to Casablanca.

NUMBERS

HATEVER the motives were that impelled Uncle Melech toward Casablanca, his instincts were sound. I, too, that first day, fell in love with this beautiful city of the Moghreb el Aksa which, arrayed in all the colors of Islam, stands mirroring itself in the mirror of Atlantic. As upon some Circean strand magical with voices, I could have halted my travels there; indeed, it was music, a singing that issued like silken colored thread from the door of a café hard by the Hotel des Ambassadeurs, where I had just registered for my initial Arabian night, that first snared me, enchanted me to enter, and there held me entangled in the nostalgia of its distant Oriental evocations.

The words of the young Arab's song I could not make out at all, save here and there a few Semitic vocables that spoke to me as through a latticed window—*ward* for flower, *hawah* for love. It was the music, however, its minor key, its gesticulative cadence, that bowed to me, that touched lips and forehead to me, that greeted me with salaam-shalom, that with cantorial trills and tremolos self-infatuated made holiday for me, rising, as the singer swooned, to paradisiac fields, falling, descending, lingering recitative upon a middle path, and finally with meditative mournfulness coming to rest, with sob, with sigh. I recognized in that singing the accents of forgotten kinship and was through it transported back to ancient star-canopied desert campfires about which there sat, their faces fire-lit, my ancestors and that Arab's.

The singer was followed by a story-teller, a bearded, wrinkled man, cowled in his burnous, an ape's mischief twinkling from his eyes, who, speaking a strange sun-baked French, regaled his audience with tales of wonder and innuendo. The story of *The Seven Angles of the Yashmak*, whose telling was accompanied by much coy pantomime, set the café roaring; *The Stutterer's Parrot*, too, was a kind of *tour de force* in which Arabic, Berberi, and French stumbled over one another to the great delight of his listeners, whose appreciation was obviously profounder than mine; but it was his *Tale of the Ethiopian Who Did Change His Skin* that was most seriously received and most loudly applauded. This was a fable of an unlucky-lucky Negro whose skin changed with the changing of the seasons: in the summer he was black, black as coal; in the autumn he turned brown, henna-brown; in winter he was yellow; and in the spring he blossomed white. Summer he was black again. It was an engaging anecdote pointing many a moral, and suffused throughout with a sense of the possible-marvelous. The story-teller, moreover, exploited to the full the absurdities of the fourfold dilemma, telling of the Ethiopian's troubles with his wife, who one spring day found that her husband had faded, of the confusion he caused to functionaries who as they registered him brown looked up to see him yellow, and of the pied and measled aspect that was the Ethiopian's one June day when it hailed.

I fell asleep that night to the singing of the young Arab, wafted across the street to the open balcony of my room; but I slept fitfully—it was hot, the very pillows seemed to sweat—and when I did fall off in sleep, I tossed and tossed, disturbed, I think, by the call of old-new affinities, nightmared by the tall Sudanese who paced my dreams, veiled in a yashmak, stuttering.

When I had arrived at Casa it had been too late to go to the office of the JDC, but on the following morning I was there early. It was closed: *fête nationale*. Well, I had waited thirty years to see Uncle Melech; I could wait one day more.

So I spent the rest of that day renewing my courtship of the city, which, despite its imposed Gallic quiddities, shimmered of the East, and whose minarets, like flutes, charmed away all that of the Occident still clung to me. Wandering along boulevards named after French marshals and along side streets that remembered quietly mullahs and sultans dethroned, I mingled with the crowd. Everything was a fascination, rich, crayoned. After the drabness and austerity of the Italian camp, after the wan bleached faces among whom I had spent my life up to now, this was cornucopia and these people an arc of the rainbow of race. I lingered in the markets and souks, my eyes luxuriating upon each opulent still life displayed on barrow or heaped up behind the windows of the cool marble-slabbed arcades—the golden oranges of Tetuán, pyramided; naveled the pomegranates of Marrakech; Meknes quince; the sun sweet inside their little globes, and upon their skins the mist of unforgotten dawns, the royal grapes of Rabat. Even the sheathed onions, mauve, violet, pink, poll-tufted like the warriors of the Atlas, seemed fruit that I had never seen before. And dominating—whether in the cool smooth round or, sliced, as crimson little scimitars adorning the Negro smile—were watermelons, miniature Africas, jungle-green without, and within peopled by pygmy blacks set sweetly in their world of flesh.

The morning passed as upon a flowered dial, and at noon, what with the irresistible fruit, and the lemonade sipped under awnings, there was no desire in me for food. I had been sustained by the richness of scene, by sound, by the pollen of perfume, for in this realm he is a great man, the apothecary, raising with powdered thumb, summoning through the triturated drop the ghosts of roses, the seven-veiled shadows of the jasmine. When I did pause before the entrance of a restaurant—not so much to read the menu as to admire the magnificence of the Senegalese doorman, tall obelisk in basalt, his cheeks with concentric carmine scars carved—the odor of oil and the gorging at all tables, a rite of grossness and plump-fingered delicacy, stifled whatever appetite I had had. Upon another occasion and in a more ascetic environment I might have been tempted by these succulent chickenwings that here made dripping mustaches for the round Levantine in a fez, or by the mounds of saffron and rice, or even the cubed sheep's meat glistening fat. There were, too, the classics of the French cuisine, to whose napoleonic strategy my palate had ever surrendered—but the gourmandizers repelled me. They lived well, these Moors; but too well: the thigh-filled pantaloons that waddled along the street; the Negress with scarves, striped as with the lines of latitude, knotted about her large hips, gripping a sausage in her inkish-pink palm; the paunch-proud merchant seating his buttock and belly on his chair—these spoke eloquently of past banquets, of many-coursed meals digested reposeful upon soft pillows and divans beneath the gauze of golden slumber, the brocade of the gold snore.

I ordered some white sugarcakes, drank my little cups of Turkish, and was once again among the gaunt-faced Berbers in bright caftans, the French bureaucrats colonial-correct, the linen tunics, the calico and the muslin.

It was, however, the everywhere-encountered art of smiths, builders, and craftsmen that won back my admiration and in its shapes and forms dovetailed and mortised into the welcoming hollows of my heart. Like the music I had heard the night before, this was an art of traceries and fretwork where both space and space filled, combined and embraced, interlaced, wove out of iron or the inscribed stone their flowing arabesques: *Neskhi*, the calligraphy of growing things, pattern of shoot and tendril and climbing vine: a virtuosity it was of curlecue and flourish curving gracefully in the tall arched portal or delicately run to shape the cinctured dome: an art of alternations and changes where the white marble gave way to black, the black to white, twins of symmetry in polite accommodating dance; a discipline of design, yet a playfulness, the artist abstracting—may his shadow never diminish!—abstracting the beauty of the world to its planes and lines, rolling in intimate involvement the intertangled triangles, the paired squares; eschewing image, delighting in form; *Kufi,* the very pilgrims of the script, staff-bearing, marching; and everywhere, whether through the cursive, which is like a sultan at ease, or through the angular, which is like a sultan in state, filling my soul with remoteness, with remoteness made familiar and near.

It was not difficult for me to understand, stirred as I was by these inarticulate nostalgias, the sense of at-homeness that in past centuries entire communities of Jews—scholars, goldsmiths, potters, silk-weavers, sandalmakers, minters, poets—had felt dwelling here in the domain of the maariv. I, too, found myself as in some palmettoed atrium to the Holy Land. But all that day, among faces that continually suggested but never asserted their Semitism, I did not meet a Jew.

My visit the next morning to the rue Gallieni was again a frustration. *Monsieur le Directeur,* I was informed, was away at Oujda and might perhaps be back the next day.

"Can I do anything for you?" The matronly person in charge of the office put into her question both the natural politesse of her French speech and the proverbial hospitality of her Sephardic origin.

"I am looking for a Melech Davidson."

"Monsieur Davidson?" She regarded me suspiciously. Her cordiality of the moment before vanished; she turned back to her fellow employees, staring at us, attentive, and I got the impression of a secret shared.

"Monsieur Davidson is parted. He's not here any more." She looked finality.

"Do you know where I could reach him?"

"He's not here, he's not more at Casablanca."

"But—"

"He was here, but he's been expulsed"—she hadn't intended to say it—"he's been expulsed from the region."

"What for?"

"I believe, monsieur, that you had better speak to Monsieur le Directeur. This is not in our department. Moreover, we do not know who you are. We have had enough trouble. Truly, we do not care to discuss the *affaire* of—of the mullah of the mellah?"

The girls tittered.

"I beg your pardon?"

"Monsieur le Directeur will be able to give you all the informations you search. I am not informed. . . . I am not authorized."

There was no point in pressing the conversation further. I would not let go, however, of that last word of hers. Tourist-like, I asked:

"Is there a mellah here?"

"*Mais, oui!* And what a mellah! *Le mellah des mellahs!* Would you care"—guide-like she volunteered—"to visit it? Our chauffeur, Monsieur Dauphin, will be pleased to direct you."

She sent a young doe-eyed stenographer to go look for him.

"And ah, yes, we can oblige you. A photograph of your Monsieur Davidson—to solace your disappointment, and"—she smiled—"to atone for our reticence. Not a very good one, but something so that from our office you go not away empty-handed."

All my life I had waited for this picture, and now at last I was to see him, Uncle Melech plain!

She handed me the snapshot.

It showed a man standing in the midst of a group of barefooted boys. But his face—Uncle Melech had again eluded me. It was a double, a multiple exposure!

As I slid the snapshot into my wallet, M. Dauphin appeared. The chauffeur—may Allah be praised for the world's chauffeurs, they preserve the art of conversation—was an extrovert, and loquacity itself. Sitting in the jeep that was to take us the half-dozen blocks to the ghetto, he was at once autobiographical, historical, critical, geographical, and wise. His ancestral name had originally been *Dalfen,* but disliking the connotations of penury that flowed from the Hebrew word, he had had it changed to Dauphin, and felt consequently more French if not more princely. His grandfather, he recalled, had dwelt in the mellah, but through a series of fortunate events had lifted himself in the social scale, and now the grandson could serve a great organization like the Zhaydaysay and live in Casablanca proper, which vaunted these charming esplanades and these hotels ten stages high and the American movies (I had sat in one of them the night before, the film had been of the issue of 1945, and the newsreel had shown Churchill still poising the world upon forked fingers) and all modern conveniences, perhaps almost like New York.

Suddenly across a boulevard upon which there fronted a most impressive hotel—the Dauphin's pride —suddenly against walls such as those upon which circus posters are posted, we came upon the mellah.

"With a car it is impossible to traverse. Too strait."

We parked off the boulevard and proceeded on foot. We entered, we slid into the mellah; literally: for the narrow lane which gaped through the gateway at the clean world was thick with offal and slime and the oozing of manifold sun-stirred putrescences; metaphorically: for in a moment we knew that the twentieth century (with all its modern conveniences) had forsaken us, and we were descending into the sixteenth, the fifteenth, twelfth, eleventh centuries. The streets, narrow and mounting, mazed, descending and serpentine, formicated with life. Everywhere poverty wore its hundred costumes, tatters of red and tatters of yellow, rags shredded and rags pieced, a raiment of patches, makeshifts, and holes through which the naked skin showed, a kind of human badge. Brightness, however, fell only from rags; if a garment was whole, it was black, the somber ghetto gaberdine.

Most of the people who lived in these labyrinthine hutches and warrens were out in the open: the tailor sitting upon the cobblestones, his feet under him; the housewife, caressing a vegetable; the aged, murmuring; and the blind—upon so sunny a day so many blind!—reclining against a wall waiting for tomorrow against a wall to recline. At one strategic corner eighteen of these heaps of helplessness, wrapped in rags and white-pupiled blindness, were counted.

Up and down the streets, a water-carrier, panniered like a beast of burden, walked with a singular air of self-importance.

As we made our way with difficulty through the congested lanes, avoiding a body here, evading a donkey there, we were everywhere beset—by hands! Wherever we turned—hands! I was reminded of those drawings illustrative of Dante's *Inferno* in which the despair of its denizens is shown rising from the depths in a digitation and frenzy of hands, hands snatching at straw, at air, at hands. This was a population of beggars greeting me with outstretched palms, with five-fingered plea. I was making acquaintance with the civic gesture of the mellah of Casablanca.

Over the protest of my guide, who informed me

that if I began this thing there would be no end to it —there were twenty-five thousand who lived here— I distributed the largesse of my Moroccan small change and made to go on my way. It was impossible; I was prevented; for there at my feet was the grateful recipient, blessing me with all the blessings that the richness of his imagination and the poverty of his state could command, salaaming before me, and finally, prostrate, smiting his forehead thrice upon the ground. I had not realized the intent of these abasements until they were over. Embarrassed, ashamed, yet angry for the innocence of my shame, I hastened forward.

It is a figure of speech, this hastening; for here one cannot hasten. One battles one's way through the ambush of petition, one pushes cruelly forward. At the same time one must be careful of one's footing; there is commerce here!—and the refuse of commerce. Here, behind his veil of flies, is a butcher; he has for sale one pendulous hooked piece of liver; he stands before it, fanning it; the flies would bankrupt him. Yonder his competitor does better, he sells tripe; and for tripe there are customers. Fish are for sale today, too; the guts of fish, blood and pale balloon, lie in the roadway alongside which the seven-scummed runnels slowly flow in filthy arabesque. Upon the cobbles of the streets, everywhere, the marks of trade-rubbish, rottenness, the signs of a donkey's passage.

In their booths, standing dark and æsthetic behind their colored quantums of spice, the spice-venders. Puzzled, I asked M. Dauphin who were the customers who bought these luxuries.

"It is not of luxe at all," he said. "Spice is a great stifler of hunger. It deceives the stomach; it induces a belief that a banquet has been had when only a morsel has been eaten. The spice-venders, these *bnai-attar,* are here a venerable guild."

We came upon another group of beggars, idols in the sun, dreaming of the vizier's ingots.

"You see that mendicant over there?" asked M. Dauphin pointing to a blind, filthily draped, bag-o'-bones hag. "She is unique in the mellah. Not unique in that she is blind and deaf-mute, there are many of such; not even unique in that she has an assistant, the blindness often compels such organization; but unique in the place she inhabits. She has no home, not even one of these hovels; but there at the side of that house is a kennel. Into it her assistant pushes her, and, as circumstances require, withdraws."

Now, not even in Canada is poverty mythical, but such wretchedness—I could not believe it real. Some magician out of the *Arabian Nights,* I thought, had cast upon me a spell and conjured up with sinister open-sesame this melodramatic illusion. Or perhaps it was a desert mirage that was playing tricks with my vision. Or I was dreaming, I was imagining.

Or some Hollywood producer had come here to stage a frightful scene.

But it was real. There was an element that confirmed reality.

The stench!

The odor of the centuries hovers over the mellah and will not dissipate. Not all the breezes of the Atlantic, less than a mile away, have yet effected a purification. It is an odor palpable and pervasive. Escape therefrom there is not; flight into a side alley but changes its intensity, not its nature or gust. It is, at times, an odor of nuances; an odor, also, of thick heavy undertones. Only occasionally, as when upon the air there are wafted some few motes of the pulver of spice, only then are there subtleties for the nostrils; all, otherwise, is miasma and reek. The fishheads scattered beneath the booths give off their peculiar smell; the viands, too, send up their intimations of ptomaine; there is a touch of the rancidity of dairies; garbage and refuse steam mephitic on the ground. Through the fanfare of stenches it is only the very sensitive who can distinguish the special contribution of the cat carcass drying in the sun. Yet it is not a composition without a theme; again and again, in the intervals between the abatement of one rankness and the rise of another, there is sensed the presence of the major offensiveness. It is that of ordure and dregs. Decades of digestion raise their disgust through the streets. There is no water in the mellah. The mellah's alleys are its cloaca.

Squeamish Westerner, I had to stop in my tracks. I could not proceed farther through this worst of augean stables, one which mangered humans. I turned aside and, feigning the necessity of a handkerchief, sought refuge in its clean laundered smell.

As I stood there trying to control a hypercritical gorge, M. Dauphin found my plight very amusing. "This is nothing," he said; "you should consider the condition of Jews in those Moslem countries which are unimproved by our civilization."

At that word, it almost came up. "Isn't there a place around here where I can breathe? A public building? A synagogue?"

"But certainly."

"Then let's go."

M. Dauphin turned up a side street and we passed through an open courtyard where a woman was emptying slops. "The water's last waterfall," said M. Dauphin. "First it is used for drinking, then for washing the fingers before eating, then for dishes, then for clothes, then for flushing."

"But there is plenty of water in Casablanca, is there not? Across the boulevard in the hotel there is hot and cold running water, all the time, and to spare. Why does the flow of civilization stop here at the gates of the mellah?"

"I do not know, monsieur. Perhaps it is too costly to bring water here. Perhaps it is necessary that there should be three categories of convenience: one for the metropole where live the French functionaries, one for the medina, the Arab slum, and one for the mellah where live the Jews. The French Government has much trouble often to keep the Arabs and Berbers pleased with the benefits which it has brought them; I am told that the fact that there are Jews who are very much in worse condition than they are helps toward their contentment. I do not know. But this at least is true: Jews are much better off here than among other Moslem populations—there are, you know, almost a million Jews living under Moslem rule—and better off now than when I was a little boy. Then no Jew was allowed to walk on the sidewalk as an Arab passed; no Jew was permitted to mount a horse—a horse, it is an animal noble—no Jew was permitted to mount a donkey, for then he would have been looking down on the Arab. And plus, it was prohibited that he wear white; black he had to wear, the color of indignity, and even to this day you can distinguish, despite their common swarthiness, Arab from Jew by their headgear: a black skullcap is a Jew. It was bad. I mention only the outer signs of discrimination, the mood of the country, its atmosphere. When a Moslem had to bring the word *Jew* into his conversation, he would apologize, as for a pornography;

I do not detail the actual injustice and oppression. Some of the disabilities still remain, but the French have effected veritable progress. Moreover, monsieur, these people do not feel as sad about their condition as you do. The evil has also brought its own alleviation—they, too, have been infected by Islam's submissiveness. Ask one of them how he stands it and he will no doubt answer: *Katoob!* It is written. It is written; he accepts."

We had reached the synagogue, and here, too, there were the usual paupers, lying on the steps, intoxicated with the hashish of *katoob*. The synagogue was cool and airy and afforded a pleasant relief from the swarming, stifling out-of-doors. There adorned it the customary Judaic symbols. Hanging from the base of the menorah, however, was a shaped metal hand; the design recurred throughout the synagogal ornamentation. I pointed to it, inquiringly.

"The hand of Fatima," said M. Dauphin. "For good luck."

M. Dauphin, apparently, was not pleased with my reaction to this novel ecclesiastic appurtenance. "You remind me," he said, "you remind me very much of the last man I guided through the mellah. He wasn't precisely a visitor, he came from arriving to Casa to take up his duties with our organization and I was instructed to conduct him through the mellah. He, too, was nauseated, he actually rejected.

And you should have heard him on Fatima, on the water question, on *katoob*. He moved even me, truly. When he came back to the office he was practically in tears, clutching at his bearded jowls, pacing up and down, forgetting altogether that he was a subordinate. To think of it, he kept exclaiming: 'These are Jews! Jews whose forefathers were once the dons and hidalgos of the golden age of Spain! Jews whose ancestors were once counselors and advisers to caliphs, to kings, whose writ ran current through the land, who are of the true blood, the unbroken lineage! Go see them now! Once their sires sat in the seats of justice, judging, whose scions now stand at the gates of the mellah begging! Impossible! Impossible! Morocco, Fez, Tetuán—these were names once glorious in our annals, seats of learning, sanctuaries of Torah! Now they are the prisons of untouchables. Casablanca, Casablanca, beautiful Casablanca, where Churchill and Roosevelt planned the triumph of our civilization—I spit!' M. Davidson was a very hysterical man."

"But not a man in error."

I tried to be as casual as I could, I remembered the taciturnity of the office. "Surely his anger was justified."

"Perhaps, but he caused us much trouble. We have to be co-operative with authority. We could not get very far with critique. Monsieur le Directeur, I can assure you, feels just as sensitively about the whole thing as did this Davidson. But to make scenes! That only makes us retrogress. . . . We sent him into the mellah to gather up statistics for us. He was in fact very efficient and brought us back the calculations. He showed, for example, that the death rate was among males fifty per cent in thirteen years; there are no official records, but Monsieur Davidson compared the names in the book of circumcision with the names in the book of *bar mitzvahs* and found half missing. He brought us statistics on blindness, on trachoma, on ringworm of the scalp, on itches, scabs, and young boys' baldness. He made us a graph of the incidence of tuberculosis, a tall black chart. All this was very useful, it helped us make our plans, settle our appropriations. But then what do you think he did? He sat down and wrote a letter to the editor of *Le Maroc* in which he made public all the facts and figures he had collected and ironized about the triple slogan of the French Revolution!" *

"That didn't bring any reforms?"

"That didn't bring any reforms. The letter wasn't even published! The editor telephoned the *directeur* and we had to make explanations and apol-

* Uncle Melech had also planned a milder form of protest. In one of the training schools of the mellah I later was given the manuscript of a one-act play that Uncle Melech had hoped to put on for the special edification of the worthies of the metropole. See *Gloss Dalid*, page 151.

ogies. For in all our efforts the Government is very helpful. It facilitates our good works. It does not even hinder our program of emigration to Israel, which is assuming greater proportions every day. As much as possible, the Government is very sympathic. Naturally, it does not want to chicane with the natives. Our Monsieur Davidson, of course, was reprimanded. But that didn't stop him. Oh no, not him. He created yet another incident. The authorities, you will understand, are very concerned over the good repute of Casa, it is a modern French city, they do not wish begging in the streets. They pass, therefore, very severe ordinances to suppress the mendicancy. Anyone convicted of begging in the streets is sent for eight days to the pond—an open enclosure in the desert without shelter from the sun. Very incomfortable. Now one day a group of them, Jews, are sent away. They are there three days, four days, five days. Monsieur Davidson then commences organization. He is very popular in the mellah, the beggars have faith in him, they follow his counsel; so in the dead of night he leads a whole company of them, armed with sticks, stones, and other weapons, out into the desert. *Le Maroc* described it the next day: 'a horde of beggars, the halt, the crippled, the dumb, the blind, led by the blind led by the maimed, and Davidson at their head!' The pond has only one guard, a Negro, who, catching sight of the grotesque and threatening crew, runs away. The freed beggars are brought back to the mellah. . . . Naturally Davidson is arrested."

"And sent to the pond?"

"Almost. It was an affair of scandal—in our office we do not care to talk about it—but Monsieur le Directeur interceded for him, and we succeeded in having the accusation broken. He was, however, demissioned from his post. He was, in fact, sent with our last boatload to Marseille, from there they proceed, or already have proceeded, to Israel."

We had reached the gate of the mellah and the long, broad palm-sentineled boulevard. One could breathe again.

I did not go back the next day to the rue Gallieni. I knew what I had wanted to know. I was eager to leave the city where the word Jew was a term of pornography, eager to leave it and its false music, its hollow art, eager to shake from my feet the dust of this city of the teated domes and the phalloi of minarets.

DEUTERONOMY

HE FLIGHT to Israel, from the moment when we rose over the Mediterranean to the moment when the plane banked and the land lay before us like an open slanted Bible, was a smooth going through space above calm dozing leviathans of water and over clouds, herds of white horses, maned, rounded, rampant.

Warmed by the sun beating through the porthole, my mind was dreamily in communion with the murmur of the motors humming through aluminum. They made me whatever music my mind willed, ululative, messianic, annunciatory. It was as if I was part of an ascension, a going forward in which I was drawn on and on by the multiple-imaged appearing and disappearing figure of Uncle Melech.

Not entirely self-induced my dreams and exaltations were; they were, in a way, the result, I think, of the broken tangential conversation with which the man who sat beside me sought to while away the hours. I never did discover his name or calling, I gathered only that he was a sort of journalist, member of an assimilated Jewish family and of recent years an enthusiast of the Zionist movement. He repeatedly apologized for the inadequacy of his Jewish background—he did indeed know more about the Tarot cards than about the Torah scroll—but he felt that this—he nodded east—was the greatest thing that had happened in Jewish history in a long time and he wanted to feel himself part of it.

He had, moreover, a theory about contemporary events, and it was the exposition of this theory —broken by deviations, by distractions, words uncaught or words misunderstood because of the noise —that carried us to the very airfield at Lydda. It ran as a vague accompaniment to my own inward thoughts, at times harmonizing with them, at times rudely dispelling.

The miracle of miracles for Christians, he asserted, was the miracle of the Incarnation. We Jews, however, had refused to surrender our belief to it because, among other reasons, we ourselves had exemplified through the centuries an opposite miracle. The Judaic Idea, he explained, had come into the world concretized in the customs and thoughtways of the Hebrews, garbed, as it were, in the vesture of chosen Israel. In a world of barbarism and idolatry it had been the Jewish nation that had been the dwelling-place of the Immanence of Deity. With loss of homeland and of national sovereignty, however, the Idea had been banished. It lost Its local habitation and in a sense Its name; It doffed the flesh that had been Its first abode. Yet It persisted. It was the miracle of the Discarnation.

It was true, the man conceded, that the Jews qua Jews—the tatters of that original divine vestment, the shreds of the flesh that once showed forth the Lord—had recognizably remained. But not as of yore: they no longer served in their first role, they were not any more the Idea's style and title. They had been reduced to but a single function: mnemonic of the past. Upon the face of the earth stationed as scarecrows, they frighted away the devouring fowl not because of what they were, but because of what they resembled.

Jewry had ceased as Existence. Among the nations it constituted an anomaly, in speech it was a solecism: the verb *to be* confined to the passive mood!

But through its early influence upon the civilizations and religions of the world—above all, through its ineluctability as Absolute—the Judaic Idea continued. It continued as Essence. Without home, yet everywhere; without language, yet echoed in all speech; without polity, yet the inspiration and basis of all social contract, the Idea prevailed. It went forth as exile; it remained—conqueror.

The consequences of this separation of Essence from its typical Existence, the man elaborated, were early apparent. Jewry, leading in the lands of the Diaspora but a vestigial part-existence, moved of necessity between banality and suffering. Suffering, indeed, became the index of its viability, the mirror fogged at the seemingly breathless mouth. Jewry ceased to consider life as a reality to be experienced, but as a gantlet to be run. The secret of the run gantlet is to reduce yourself to as small a size as possible. Jewry turned inward.

In its flight from suffering, in its search for escape from its unexalted diurnalities, its sæcular pedestrianism—the philosopher paused in approbation of the word, which at once connoted mediocrity and wandering—Jewry still further ghettoized itself. It lost itself in the contemplation of the One; with commentary hooped upon commentary it constricted Him until from Circle He diminished to Dot.

Jewry ceased to be of Time. History with its many chariots thundered by on all sides. Jewry stood patient, passive.

And then, suddenly, this extra-temporal nonexistence leaped back into Time and Reality! What had impelled the leap?

It was, the man answered, an awareness that

the specter-people was immune to death. This had been proved empirically; Jewry could not wholly die. This knowledge, moreover, had been more than a mere consolation; it had turned into a path of life. In the light of this truth, the chance involved in seeking a Return to Time could now be taken, since it did not at all involve taking a chance; nothing could be lost. Hence the leap—he was now all triumph and elation—the leap from mere Existence back to Essence. It was thus that he had seen Israel in one single saltation leap from the marginalia of Europe back to the center and body of its past and future. Whether the Essence now before us would be of the same transcendence and glory as that of the past remained to be seen. This was one of the reasons for his own journey to Israel. One thing, however, was certain: pulverized, etherealized Jewry had put on flesh again. It was our version of the Incarnation.

Though the man's thesis ran as counterpoint to my own reflections, sending me in the intervals between statement and development on private messianic search, I could not refrain from taking issue with many of his assertions. They seemed to me to be too facile, too glib; his novelties were largely verbalizations; there was much that his theory too gallantly ignored. We were still catechizing the matter when we found ourselves before the customs wicket at Lydda.

"And what role," I asked (I really wanted to know), "does Providence play in your scheme? You have forgotten, in your thesis, to place God."

He may have had some good excuse for his oversight, but I never did hear it, for at this moment the customs officer summoned him. I was myself called away, and the last I saw of the man was as he stood there in front of the officer declaring his camera and, perhaps, his God, the customs officer smiling.

My sojourn in Israel was a continual going to and fro, an unremitting excitement. I wanted to take in the whole country, all at once. If a plane had been available I should have loved to have risen in it so that I might look at Dan and Beersheba simultaneously. If I could only stretch out my arms and make them the land's frontiers! For there wasn't a place, disguised though it might be under a latter-day name, that didn't speak to me out of my personal past. Even as I arrived in Lydda, there came to me the memory of those winter evenings in Montreal when, as a boy of thirteen, I had gone through the tractate *Baba Bathra,* pausing in young wonder at the mathematical ingenuity of the famous merchants of Lud, whose shrewd manipulation of percentages had caused so much concern to the sages of the Talmud. It was the same, it was intenser, in the case of the other cities of Israel—Carmel-crowning Haifa, idyllic Tiberias, Jerusalem ineffable. I kept motoring by bus, by taxi, by jeep provided by the Jewish Agency, from one part of the country to the other, now spending a day in the desert southlands, now resting at Beersheba (oh, the heat and the beelzebub flies!), then issuing forth to look from a distance at Gaza and its mosque, where alien Egyptians regretted Pharaoh in his tomb; turning back again to murmurous Tel Aviv; sleeping a night at Ain Harod, where the moon shone like a gong on the balcony of the guest-house; at Nazareth, in front of the two oleanders of the Church of the Annunciation, blossoming; north to within sight of Mount Hermon; south again—how I longed for the gift of ubiquity! Only thus, I began to think, would I be able to accomplish my twofold mission: the discovery, among Israel's speeches, proclamations, fervors, grumblings, and hopes, of the country's typical poetic statement, and the recognition—the word was acquiring for me more and more of its Greek connotation—the recognition of Uncle Melech.

The JDC, I learned the very first day I was at Tel Aviv, no longer considered Uncle Melech its special protégé. He was no longer in its employ. Immediately upon his arrival he had gone out on his own. He was somewhere in Israel, but where they could not tell. I soon realized that I had imposed on myself an almost impossible task. Find Uncle Melech! Among the thousand thousands of Jews come from all corners of the earth, scattered now in cities and in settlements, many still living in tents—in tents with addresses!—multitudes of them still unregistered and lost among the anonymities who had pierced through and evaded the coastal guard that during recent years had stood with flaming sword to prohibit access to sanctuary—multitudes severing their last connections with the exilic past, boasting newly Hebraized names, a grand casting for the roles of the Bible—multitudes moving from one part of the country to another, either with the army or upon the civilian projects of irrigation, road-building, house-construction—among these fluctuating and protean multitudes to look for Uncle Melech was to suspect him everywhere and to find him nowhere.

I didn't know where to begin. I thought at first that Uncle Melech's experience at Casa might have impelled him toward the Yemenite or Sephardic sections of Tel Aviv. I did make inquiries there, but I learned only of their own felicity. How Uncle Melech would have rejoiced to see them as I had that Sabbath morn seen them, the bearded dark-eyed little men, their delicate gazelle-like daughters, pacing with staid dignity down the streets of the city on their way to the service at the synagogue! Changed they were, and altered, transformed, not untouchables, but princes and princesses in a colored book, though now in Israel they were bearers of burdens, stevedores, newsies, elevator-boys (whose houses but a year ago must needs be lower than the lowest Arab's!), the mellah look gone from them, and they at last, at last robed in *white*, white for the Sabbath of their week, and for the Sabbath of their lives—white!

But Uncle Melech was not to be identified among these.

I sought him in the Quarter of the Hundred Gates in Old Jerusalem, in its winding, chaffering streets, its ancient courtyards, in the shabby rooms of charity-supported academies, among the gaunt fasters and the Talmud students of the corkscrew earlocks; and there again—though often I thought I descried his mellah stance a street away—he eluded me.

There was a man riding a donkey on Julian's Way who bore a faint resemblance to the blur on my snapshot; but he was from Salonika.

I was with the venerable elders of Jerusalem as they went forth on the eve of Tisha B'Av to weep on Mount Zion for the holy city whose memorials and ancient stones were still in the hands of the invader, sobbing for that the Western Wall and the Temple site, the shrines, the tombs, still stood unredeemed, and even access to the cherished ruins was still impossible:

> *The splendour and richesse of alle Spain*
> *Y-wis it is a smal thing in mine eyn*

93

Whan that I long for to behold agayn
Even the pore duste of thy shende shrine!

In mournful broken singsong they read from the archaic Zionides of Rabbi Yehuda Ha-Levi and from the Lamentations; and their voices were almost female with pathos; I would have sworn it was my mother's voice, as it used to sound, humble, imploratory, when by rote she recited her sad liturgies. Would Uncle Melech's voice, I wondered, on this occasion resemble hers? But soon I, too, was tearful among the mourners.

I went to the *moshavim,* the *kibbutzim,* settlements that were like flourishing oases, outposts that were like barracks of the French Foreign Legion. Surely Uncle Melech, ever zealous for new ideological experiment and frontier, would sense their attraction! I talked to chalutzim, old settler and new adept, and in their dedication to the soil and their scorn of the possessive pronouns detected many a phrase that might have come out of an amalgam of Uncle Melech's ethical and devotional vocabularies.

Hoping by accident to stumble upon his name, I made a habit of picking up roll-calls, lists of refugees, official records, anything that might produce the fortunate find. Half in curiosity and half in expectation I would go through these catalogues of incognitos; they were all alike; Uncle Melech was nowhere listed, yet each name somehow seemed his alias. Lazarus Achron; Israel Agathides; Yerachmiel Alkudsi; Moishe Anav; Chatzkel Belfer; Isac Chamouche; Ibrahim ibn Daoud; Shloime Evyan; Enoch Fried; Jonah Furchtiger; Jacob Gottlieb; Samuel Galut; M. Hadom; Pinchas Hasdi; I. Iota; Kalman Klain; Abraham Nistar; Yidel Nebich; Elijah Razin; Simon Rachmin; Luis de Santangel; B. Schweig; I. I. Segal; Immanuel Shemantov; Menachem Taimon; Hans Taub; Boris Trizatchest; Leopold Untertahn; Dov Vives; Alter Vital; Noah Venod; Aaron Wassertrager; Saul Xenos; Ephraim Zacuta; Henri Zadoc; Jochanan Zefany—they seemed endless, tantalizingly familiar, yet forever elusive.

Everyone at some time, I was told, must cross the Mograbi, the central square of Tel Aviv, peripatesis and boardwalk of all its philosophies. I placed myself at this Cartesian vantage point and watched the policeman on his cement elevation directing the traffic with gestures reminiscent of the blessing of the Sabbath candles. As on all sides groups of pedestrians pushed and crushed toward their several destinations, their talk always an identification, I wondered in which of these eddies Uncle Melech might be found. Among the Moroccan fatalists? Among the blond Germans, positivists, politely asseverating *ja* and *ja-wohl?* Among the resourceful eclectic Poles? Or perhaps here at my side among the Bulgarian fundamentalists, crosslegged eager bootblacks? Perhaps this group of Johannesburgers, pragmatic and reserved, concealed his presence? Or maybe the hard glottic accents I heard before me, which in my mind I designated *sabra,* were those of Uncle Melech? Such transformations had happened before: the immigrant of a fortnight ago as indigenous as the seventh-generation Palestinian. This well might be the long-sought voice. I looked in its direction; it belonged to another of those many men in Israel, past middle age and not bald, who looked like Ben-Gurion, so fuzzy, white, and electric was their hair.

Had Uncle Melech, perhaps, become a devotee of Tel Aviv's sidewalk cafés, rendezvous of Israel's mighty talkers, public refuge of its solitary letter-writers? Often as I sat on the terraces of this non-alcoholic Paris, my curiosity dwelling on this Jew lost in his epistolary dilemma, or that one, excited, gesticulating his cause (even in the days of the Psalmist it was held that if the right hand lost its cunning, the tongue would cleave to the roof of the mouth), I thought: "Should I go over? Should I send the waiter with a note?" It was only a fancy, the notion was preposterous. Was I Israel's census-taker?

I should have thought of it before, but often the obvious escapes us—an ad in the newspapers. There appeared, therefore, in the *Palestine Post* and in *Davar* prominent little boxes announcing that a relative, Melech Davidson, formerly of Ratno and

Kamenets, was being sought by his nephew, who could be reached at the Hotel Ha-Yardain. It was not until the third day that a man presented himself, a blue-eyed, frank-faced person, who didn't seem to know what to do, whether to rush forward at me and embrace me, to burst out crying, or formally to introduce himself. He formally introduced himself. We sat opposite each other and talked, but unfortunately he knew very little about himself, Melech Davidson, except that he was from Ratno and Kamenets. He spoke Yiddish, but it wasn't the Yiddish of my parents; it sounded rather like—there was so little Hebrew in it, and it shot from his throat so gutturally—rather like German. It was without reluctance that I dismissed him. Whether he was, as I put him down to be, one of those Germans stranded in the Middle East who deemed Israel the best of hiding-places, or some other seeking a visa to Canada or an immediate hand-out, he was not Uncle Melech.

Yet the feeling that I was missing him by an arm's length continually haunted me. A change in our relationship had ensued; it was he, I felt, who was now pursuing me. It hadn't been to look for Uncle Melech that I had come to Israel, my publisher had wanted a book, yet everywhere, and at the most unexpected moments, the phantom Uncle Melech rose up before me. At Haifa I meet the artist Ketter, who paints only at night, by lamplight, by candlelight, by the headlights of automobiles; I must think of Uncle Melech and his dark angelesque meditations. At Roshpina there is a farmer who places bees on his wrist to cure with stings his arthritis; this is somehow evocative of Uncle Melech. I think of Uncle Melech when at Tiberias, in the sunken dimple of the land, I sit on the terrace facing the blue of Lake Kinnereth, listening to the boatman in the gaily painted boat singing Rahel's song:

It may be these things never did occur.
Perhaps, somehow,
I never did arise at break of day
To do labor in the garden
With the sweat of my brow;

Did never, in the long and fiery days
Of harvest time,
High on the wagon laden with its sheaves,
Lift up my voice in rhyme;

Did never bathe within the blue
And quiet of your stream,
O my Kinnereth, O Kinnereth mine!
Were you, indeed? Or did I dream a dream?

Uncle Melech, present yet evanescent, before me, yet beyond—I have him and I have him not!

My quest of the essence of contemporary Hebrew poetry was beset by similar difficulty. My publisher had spoken of my trip as if it were going to be a simple flower-picking foray, a jaunt: *Go into the market-place and get me an Isaiah. Of psalmodists, bring me only the best. Cull me a canticle in the fields of En Gedi!* Alas, it was not that easy at all.

Since the death of Bialik there had risen no one in Israel to occupy his place of eminence. Fiery, explosive, bar-kochbic, the poet Uri Zvi had captured, during the days of the trouble, the imagination of the young and the daring; his hyperboles had been made into slogans; his lacerating indignation, directed alike against the hostile and the docile, had stirred the hero's courage, reddened the compromiser's shame. Himself he had been an army with banners. Now, the battle won, or at least in cessation, he was a spent brand, an outroared lion, a brand smoldering, a lion obliquely pacing, readying his next spring.

Behind him the lesser bardlings, cubs littered in Israel, imitated the maned one's yawnings and roars. They were an intractable lot, these Irgun poets, *sabra* poets, Yemenite poets, who cultivated a hard intransigence, scoffed at all delusions intellectual, adored only the soil and the gun. They hated the ghetto and its melting, paralyzing self-pity; even the unorientated DP's, fabled in their writings as Herr Flotsaum and Doktor Jetsaum, excited only their satire. In their little magazines they invariably referred to themselves as *Anachnu* (Us)—unhappy reminiscence of *nous autres, nos otros, sinn fein*—xenophobic antonym to *Haim* (Them). Not Israelis did they style themselves, but Canaanites—more aboriginal than the aborigines! And again and again they slipped into their secondary theme—*shlilath hagaluth*—the negation of the Diaspora—a conviction that Jewry abroad was doomed, whether by the uxorious embrace of assimilation or the fierce hug of anti-Semitism, doomed to disappear, if not immediately, eventually; ultimate perdition was but a matter of time.

It was an exciting kind of poetry, large-gestured, primitive, tribal, but its insularity repelled me, its reactionary mottoes stood as a wall against my enjoyment of its rich overhanging fruit. Yet this its reactionary nature functioned in my mind also as its defense; their fierceness was not inherent, but only a reaction from the experiences of exile. It would vanish. It did not belong to the essential thoughtways of our people (Uncle Melech, I was certain, would read this literature but once); it surged up only as an answer to contemporary history. It was Israel's retort to Europe, couched in Europe's language.

The tourists who were filling Israel's hotels (the one place where I did not look for Uncle Melech) also did much to keep alive the resentments on which this poetry fed. For these travelers, already objectionable in the patronizing airs they put on,

added to their unpopularity—they were the *Haim*—
by their singular incomprehension of the ideals that
were building the State. They complained about the
rationed food, and were surly, as if they, for some
special reason, ought to have been exempted from
the regime of austerity that from Lebanon to Akaba
had rendered the belch apocryphal if not obsolete.
They persisted in telling the natives how such and
such a thing was better arranged in their own countries. They photographed everything, including the
"inmates" of refugee camps, who surprised their vis-
itors by refusing to be treated as exhibits. They were
disappointed, these pilgrims, when they found that
not everyone in Israel wore sidecurls, observed the
Blue Sabbaths, prayed thrice daily; in their home
towns at the chicken dinners where they had so valiantly wrested their heritage from the hands of the
usurper, they had dreamed, apparently, of Israel as
of a great Established Synagogue devoted to an in-
cessant praying for the salvation of the souls of its
materialist benefactors.

No, this poetry was not it, not that character-
istic utterance I was searching for; it was the poetry
of prelude, of overture. This explained, perhaps, the
harsh scrapings, the dissonant attunements. The
theme, the one melodic ascendancy, I had yet to
hear.

The poets of the settlements were milder, kinder
men. Here there still flourished the lyric of senti-

ment, tender verses modeled on Jammes, Heine, Pushkin. There was a tentativeness about these rhymes, a playing of minor chords, as if the poet were gently inviting, inducing, summoning some grander utterance that as yet had failed to come. One sensed a groping toward the phrase, the line, the sentence that would gather in its sweep the sky above and the earth below and set new constellations in each. But the word did not come. The effort, however, did produce its reward—the pastoral note these many long centuries unheard in Hebrew poesy. The flowers that blossomed in these stanzas were now of a variety, the birds were named by specific names, the animals were identifiable. They were not now described, as they had been in the commentaries of the ghetto-gotten Rashi, as "a kind of bird," "a kind of animal"—poor urbanized Rashi, who knew not to tell one creature of Holy Writ from another! I remembered, as I read these verses, my visit to the Tel Aviv zoo, a visit prompted perhaps by my remembrance of Uncle Melech's gratitude to the fauna of Kamenets, and how there the leopard and the eagle and the bear, the wild goat on his stony hill, had brought alive to me the metaphors of the Bible. In adamic intimacy the poets had returned to nature; the sulphur-crested cockatoo, the golden pheasant—they called them by their names—and the marabou, amorphous, mystical, circling ever in a round.

The schools of course had each their manifestoes, assertive self-dedications to this or that high purpose. Only the orthodox *paytanim* dispensed with program notes, for their platform did not have to be set up, it was already there, a table prepared, a *Shulchan Aruch*. Their theme a continual backward-glancing to the past and their technique a pedantry of allusiveness, their work was of Moses mosaic, a liturgy, God's poetry, which is to say poetry for the Most Merciful of Readers.

But if this was what I was seeking, I already had the originals; I was seeking the tone that might yet again re-echo, not the faint echo of the long since sounded sound. These poems, they were learned, they were truly pious, but prophecy—

There was also the vogue of the young and very wise Nathan, an agile craftsman who molded the ancient speech to modern use, whose rhymes were in themselves witty, and whose wit had but one target: the iniquity of the gentiles.

Out of the transparent subterfuges of international diplomacy he made him his bitter little odes. Often, too often, he found himself constrained, so as to give his poems meaning, to preface them with epigraphs culled from newspaper headlines; the poem of a year past read, then, like a dated editorial. Cleverly written, they were none the less ephemera, their suicide was upon them at their birth. They referred to, they did not make, Occasion.

In books, in pamphlets, in published work, the great creative fiat still remained hidden. Yet I was not downcast. For me it was a gratifying surprise that there should have been published anything at all, that a people having arrived here to dig ditches and build roads and plant trees and found cities should have had the desire and made the time to woo the Hebraic muse—daughter of Israel most unaccommodating. Even more surprising was the fact that there should have been so many who could muster the skill to compose verses. Of the many thousands who had come to Israel, thousands had not known anything that resembled an education; war, terror, and flight had been their schools, they had issued analphabet in all save the lessons of life.

This situation, I confess, had stirred hopes in me of discovering the eldorado discovery: a completely underivative poet. To find the poet who knew not of books, bard without antecedents or influences, who had never read or heard another's poems, who was his own wealth, to find him and recognize the unique, the autochthonous, the primal seed—it were the very felicity of the world's first dawn!

I am still seeking him. What I did find—in Tiberias, sacred home of the punctators who had first vocalized our script—was, I think, a sort of consolation prize, a poet of an austere economy of words, a man who set out to reduce derivativeness to a minimum, seeing that he could not altogether abolish it. He, too, was a kind of punctator, a pointer, not only a writer, but a theorist of writing.

"A poem," he said, bringing forward his meager manuscript written in a hand that from a distance resembled Uncle Melech's, "a poem is not a destination, it is a point of departure. The destination is determined by the reader. The poet's function is but to point direction. A poem is not the conflagration complete, it is the first kindling. From this premise it follows that poems should be brief, laconic. Sparks. I write, therefore, poems that do not exceed one line. Sometimes, of course—it is such a difficult art—I have to extend myself to a line and a half, even two lines. It is a prolixity which leaves me discontented."

I looked eagerly toward the manuscript.

He handed me two sheets. "The complete works of," he said.

The poems were numbered and had large spaces between them. Some were marginally titled.

7. *Madness! said the deafman watching the man*
   On the podium.

Number 8 had no name:

Pity emetic and the enema, Terror.

This was followed, after a wide significant space, by three lines, two of them scratched out, headed *Survival:*

Said the seeing-eye dog with the hearing device:

The number 10 was also its title:

Oh, to be a midge on a leaf of Zohar!

He also had a poem (No. 17) called *Literature.* It read:

Out of that chambered pyramid the triliteral verb

The mummies rise . . .

Number 3, written apparently as his style was developing, boasted a title almost as long as the poem itself: *On the clearing of the swamps at Esdraelon:*

The little arrows pierced; we fevered; we pissed black.

Anopheles, his hosts!

The last on the page was *Transitional?*

The olive wreath about the sword: will the sword

Grow olives?

And then—it was after I had returned from Tiberias to Tel Aviv to attend a literary soirée—then the creative activity, archetypical, all-embracing, that hitherto I had sought in vain, at last manifested itself. Not at the soirée. In the streets, in the shops, everywhere about me. I had looked, but had not seen. It was all there all the time—the fashioning folk, anonymous and unobserved, creating word by word, phrase by phrase, the total work that when completed would stand as epic revealed!

They were not members of literary societies, the men who were giving new life to the antique speech, but merchants, tradesmen, day laborers. In their daily activity, and without pose or flourish, they showed it to be alive again, the shaping Hebrew imagination. An insurance company, I observed as I lingered in Tel Aviv's commercial center, called itself *Sneh*—after Moses' burning bush, which had burned and burned but had not been consumed. Inspired metaphor, born not of the honored laureate, but of some actuary, a man of prose! A well-known brand of Israeli sausage was being advertised, it gladdened my heart to see, as Bashan—just tribute to its magnum size, royal compliment descended from Og, Bashan's giant king. A dry-cleaner called his firm *Kesheth*, the rainbow, symbol of cessation of floods! An ice-cream organization, Kortov, punned its way to custom fissioning *kortov*, a drop, to *kor-tov*, cold and good! In my student days I had been fascinated always by that word which put an end to the irreconcilable controversies of the House of Hillel and the House of Shammai: this House would maintain *Permitted*, that House would insist *Prohibited;* a deadlock would ensue. Came then the Talmud editor and wrote *taiku, stet,* the question abides. My teacher would then go on to explain that *taiku* was really a series of initials that stood for

Tishbi yetaraitz kushioth v'abayoth, the Tishbite would resolve all problems and difficulties. Now the magic cataleptic word was before me again, in a new context, in a newspaper, the report of a football game where the score had been tied. *Taiku!*

There were dozens, there were hundreds of instances of such metamorphosis and rejuvenation. Nameless authorship flourished in the streets. It was growth, its very principle, shown in prolific action! Twigs and branches that had been dry and sapless for generations, for millennia, now budded, blossomed—and with new flowers!

It was as if I was spectator to the healing of torn flesh, or *heard* a broken bone come together, set, and grow again.

Wonderful is the engrafting of skin, but more wonderful the million busy hushed cells, in secret planning, stitching, stretching, until—the wound is vanished, the blood courses normal, the cicatrice falls off.

I had at last discovered it, the great efflorescent impersonality.

My hopes of finding Uncle Melech revived.

And this discovered poetry, scattered though it was, had its one obsessive theme. It was obsessed by the miraculous. These names and ingenuities and businesses, these artifacts of tradesmen and workers, they were but the elements, the gestures and abracadabra of the performed miracle. It was sensed everywhere—among the Yemenites to whom the news of the State established had first come like some market rumor of the advent of the Messiah as well as among the European sophisticates who veiled their credulity with rationalization.

Little David had slain Goliath? The miracle had again been repeated; against great odds, the little struggling State had withstood the onslaught of combined might.

Jaffa had seen a whale regurgitate Jonah? A company of Jews had taken over this same city whence eighty thousand Arabs had fled: Jonah regurgitated the whale!

Deborah here had sung a victory the captains could not understand? The accents of her song re-echoed still. *They fought from heaven; the stars in their courses fought against Sisera.*

As in place after place I gathered examples of the recent marvelous, the realization grew upon me that I, too, had been the witness of a miracle—the miracle of the transformed stone. It had happened in Rome. I had been wandering up and down the hilly streets of that city and suddenly I had come upon the Via Sacra. All about me there stood, or leaned, or lay on the ground, the broken pillars of the pagan temples—the Temple of Cæsar, the Temple of Castor and Pollux, the Temple of Vesta. And then, without warning, I had found myself in front of the unspeakable arch, the Arch of Titus.

I had avoided, of course, walking under that arch. Bitter enough it had been that my ancestors, at lance-point, *sub jugum,* had had to cross beneath this yoke of stone. I had scanned it, therefore, from a distance. I had walked about it, "surrounded" it, thrown it the evil eye.

Approaching closer, I had examined the bas-relief, had looked at Titus imperial in his chariot, and had smiled to think of his miserable ending, as reported by the rabbis, of the insect that through an orifice of his face had entered his brain and there had kept buzzing, buzzing, buzzing until he had gone mad and had died.

The memory was gala in my own brain, which celebrated it: Titus troubled, Titus troubled by a gnat, Titus tortured tick by tick to death, Titus by the termite tutored: tête-à-tête. . . . A consolation.

The consolation, however, had been dissipated by the spectacle imaged on the other bas-relief, where the laureled legionaries of Rome, soldier and centurion, were shown carrying away in triumph the sacred trophies of the Temple. The seven-branched candelabrum, lifted arrogantly in the air, had burned seven wounds in my eyes. The two tablets—rather that they had been shattered! And the trumpets—out of the stone they had sounded, not as aforetime the sound of jubilee, but the broken murmur, the *shvarim,* the tragic triad of wandering and suffering and exile.

Had there not glowed in my heart that fervor which had communicated itself to me from the letter that Uncle Melech had sent me from Bari, I should have been, I think, completely shattered by these sculptured taunts, this gloating in stone. I should myself have been brought to the humiliation of my forefathers. But Uncle Melech's words were with me; *When the years were ripened, and the years fulfilled, then was there fashioned Aught from Naught.* His words, his hopes, his intuition annulled and dispelled the captive spell that had held me bound. The Arch of Titus, from being a taunt, then, had become an irony, an irony directed against itself; the candelabrum, set against the new light that had been kindled across the Great Sea, had turned into satire; the trumpets, symbolic now of jubilee, really taunted Titus!

There had come then a haze before my eyes, and the miracle—Jericho's miracle—had taken place. The arch was not there! The stone had crumbled. I did not see the arch!

. . . And now in Israel the phenomenon was being made everywhere explicit. The fixed epithet wherewith I might designate Israel's poetry, the poetry of the recaptured time, was now evident. The password was heard everywhere—the miracle!

I had found the key image.

But Uncle Melech—I had just arrived at Safed, three days remained of my planned sojourn, Uncle

Melech was somewhere in Israel, and soon I should have to return without having seen him!

It was here that an act of piety spoke well for me before the *Rebono shel Olam*, Master of Coincidences. I did not want to leave Israel without having visited, for my father's sake and my mother's, Mother Rachel's tomb at Bethlehem. A kaddish intoned at that grave, I had gathered from my mother's pious talk, was of the supremest efficacy. The road to Bethlehem from Jerusalem, however, was still held by the soldiers of the Arab Legion. Yet to have left Israel without having stirred its air with the spoken names of my parents would have been most unfilial. I felt that I ought at least to arrange for a chapter of *Mishnaioth* to be read, in memory of my parents, by the students of some devout seminary.

And no better nor holier place could there be to bring my parents' greetings, failing the Western Wall and Rachel's tomb, than the Synagogue of Rabbi Isaac Luria, known honorifically as Adonenu Rabbi Izhak, the which is initialed ARI—the Lion.

It is no magnificent edifice, this synagogue of the padding lion of the Lord, but a humble house, a place of worship such as one finds in the poorer quarters of the world's ghettos. It was high noon when I entered out of the bright sun and the white roofs and terraces into the cool of the synagogue and intruded upon a scene which, I suspected, had been static against that background for centuries. The young boy, no more than thirteen, holding his heavy tome, the tractate *Baba Kama,* might have been there as of some remote century, forever unaging in the study of Torah, which is Life; and the old venerable sage, bearded like antiquity, was, as he murmured over his book of piety, a sort of anticipatory figure, an image of the boy an era hence. They seemed, surely, not of this world: the boy rapt in the analysis of some complicated *Tosfoth,* the old man seeking blear-eyed to peer behind the mysteries of the *Pamalyah shel Malah.*

They affirmed it for me, the young boy prodigy and the old man who looked like Elijah: Israel had not only returned back into Time; it still belonged to Eternity.

I hesitated to break upon their studies, but soon the elder, sensing my presence, rose from his bench to greet me. I told him what I wanted and he said that it most certainly could be arranged, not this afternoon, it was Erev Shabbos, but, God willing, on the first day of the week. Our conversation was in Yiddish, for the old man was of those who held that Hebrew would be profaned by secular use.

"From where comes a Jew?" he asked.

"From Canada."

"Canada!" He sucked at his gums. "A great distance!"

"I flew. With the airplane it is not so great a distance."

"True. . . . True. We live in Messiah's days."

"Because the world is all good? Or, *cholila,* all evil?"

"Judgments are for God. It is the Messiah's days because we see his signs and portents everywhere. Thus is it written that when the Messiah will come there will be the wonder of *kvitzath ha-derech,* the curtailment of the route. What does this mean? It means that a route which but yesterday was long and arduous suddenly becomes short and speedy. Is this not the experience of our times? Is it not the experience of the Yemenites who, located as if on another planet, as if in another century, are brought by planes to this our century and to this our planet, our country, our home, in the space of but eight hours? . . . It is written yet again that before the coming of the Messiah there would be the *chevlai yemoth ha-moshiach,* the pain and agony of the days of the Messiah. Has any generation known deeper pain and bitterer agony than our own?"

Obviously excited by his quotations, he found it difficult to keep up with his rejuvenating enthusiasms. He paused for words, he hesitated, his tongue got caught in the weave of his texts. Laboriously he continued:

"It is written also that with the coming of the Messiah there would take place the wonder of *gilgul m'choloth*. A true resurrection! The cadavers and corpses of Jewry deceased in the Diaspora would roll and strive and roll through subterranean passages, through catacomb and grave, directed all to rise at last and stand erect on the heights of Carmel, on the hillocks of the Negev, on the mountains of Galilee. This, too, we have seen. Blessed are my eyes that have seen them, the risen from the dungeons, the pursued through the undergrounds of Europe who have taken up their stand here in Israel. . . . We live in Messiah's days. Do you not see them, these signs, as well as I, an old man, do?"

I did, indeed; he but presumed me skeptical.

"Ah, if our Safed sage, our newcomer, were here to explain it to you! He makes it as plain as on the page of a book. Perhaps you will stay—but you *are* staying for the Sabbath. Good. He will be here for maariv. He has gone out to one of our religious settlements near the frontier and should be back for the Sabbath. . . ." The old man was ecstatic. "A golden tongue he has! And such learning! You should hear him discourse on the *Maaseh Breshith*, explaining how the world was made, how in the beginning there were but the six elements, *tohu, bohu,* water, wind, darkness, and the abyss, and how with the mere *Memra,* the Word made Will, all was created. And when he expounds the *Maaseh Merkabah,* it is as if the cherubim and the seraphim were with him holding up the celestial chariot, setting in motion its wheels within wheels, and you can almost see with your own eyes the composite creature, the lion, the ox, the eagle, and the human, moving in all directions at once, the brave, the plodding, the plumed, the inspired, all motion. Oh, he makes all Zohar and Bahir, brightness and light, to shine, to shine. . . ."

I knew it, even as the old man spoke, I knew it by intuition, by inner knowledge, by pentecostal visitation, by whatever name you call the secret whisperer who brings all high tidings: it was Melech Davidson, Uncle Melech. Safed was indeed auspicious for the probing of the deepest mysteries of Torah.

I issued from the cool shadowed synagogue and walked slowly back to the hotel along Safed's tortuous streets, its roofed stepped alleys. It was noon, and the streets were empty. Suddenly there began to hum through my brain an old and cherished melody—the melody of *L'cho doidi,* the song of Sabbath greeting. It was here, here in Safed, that Rabbi Solomon Halevi Alkabez, in the very darkness of his century, had composed its words of hope and consolation. The Sabbath had not yet been ushered in, the memory of this music was anticipatory, an obeisance to both the Holy Day and the Holy City. It was a felicitous memory, for it worked in me yet further recollection of my departed father—a paradise of eternal Zohar, his!—with whom, as a boy,

I had every Friday night attended the synagogue and had sung, stanza by stanza, by the cantor echoed, the sweet verses of *L'cho doidi*. Then I thought them to be a poem in praise of the Sabbath, the Sabbath queenly as opposed to the week-days, handmaiden and profane. But now the words regained their original significance; now came to me from the rebuilt places of Israel, its hamlets, its cities, the song of Rabbi Solomon Halevi Alkabez, to a melody of the Moors composed, of triumph and fulfillment:

> *O site most kingly, O royal sanctum,*
> *Arise, go forth from among your ruins!*
> *Enough your sitting in the vale of sorrow!*
> *The Lord has readied His compassion.*
>
> *Bestir you from your dust. Array you*
> *By grace of David, son of Jesse*
> *In this my people's beauteous garment!*
> *My soul, it knows redemption nearing!*
>
> *Arise! Arouse! Arise and waken!*
> *For it has come at last, the dawning!*
> *Lift up your voice your song to utter;*
> *For on you is revealed God's glory.*

When I climbed up the staircase of the hotel, I found a group of guests, tense, serious-faced, listening to the loud excited radio in the lobby. With staccato indignation the announcer was jabbing forth the details of the outrage. It had been committed at a time of truce, if not of established peace. Its victim had been unarmed. It had been perpetrated upon Israel's territory. The assailants, who were many against one, had not come forth like men, but had shot from ambush. Upon the dead body they had poured gasoline and had sought to burn it. It was only because the fire had attracted attention and Jews from a near-by settlement had rushed forward to put it out that the body was saved from complete burning. Its features were unrecognizable. The man, however, had been identified. The martyrdom of Melech Davidson was now a symbol of the Yishuv's sense of outrage. Israel would not tolerate incidents of this kind any longer. Arrangements were being made for the martyr's funeral to take place on the first day of the week. Representatives from all parts of the country and all classes of the population would be present.

The radio was turned off. Darkness was falling and the Sabbath was with us. The guests sat in silence, uttering now and again their short exclamations of anger, horror, and pity:

"The cowards!"

"Peace! Peace! There is no peace!"

"What a death!"

"Anointed, with gasoline! Anointed!"

Thus was my Sabbath turned to mourning. Across the continents I had looked and searched for my kinsman, and now that I had found him—I would not ever look upon his face. Forever would I have to bear in my mind my own conjured image of Uncle Melech.*

It was a strange funeral. In clouds of dust they came, from all parts of the country and from all classes of the population, corteges of cars and pilgrimages on foot, climbing the hills of Galilee. It was a convocation of mourning; it was also a national demonstration. As the banners and slogans were raised aloft, announcing the names of settlements in the Negev, in the Emek, in the Galil, each with its own exclamatory reaction to these obsequies which transcended their immediate purpose, it was as if the tribes of Israel had come to life again and were traveling as in olden times, each with its devices and gems: Reuben of the sardius bearing a banner gules, its device mandragora; Simeon of the topaz a banner vert, its device the city of Shechem; Levi of the stone smaragd; Judah of the emerald; Issachar of the sapphire, and Zebulun of the diamond; Dan, his banner azure with serpent couchant; Gad of the agate; of the amethyst, Naphtali; Asher of the stone of Tarshish; Joseph of the onyx, and jaspered Benjamin.

A vast congregation it was, solemn, sacerdotal,

* He left no belongings. A few sheets of manuscript, drafts for a liturgy, obviously incomplete, were his sole legacy. See *Gloss Hai,* page 189.

gathered as for some high mythic rite in which were concealed its most personal experience and its most deeply cherished verities.

There were speeches. But they were restrained, the speakers obviously fearing to indulge in flights of eloquence; the facts themselves moved mountains. In quiet tones, as if they were talking to their own souls, they spoke of Uncle Melech and of how he had become a kind of mirror, an *aspaklaria*, of the events of our time. They spoke of the influence he had already exerted upon his contemporaries, of his philosophy, of how he had through the sheer force of his existence again in our life naturalized the miracle. The company of men now he had left and was one with the soil of Israel, but here in Israel these were not really tombs but antechambers to new life, the mise-en-scène for an awakening. Dramatically one speaker pointed in the direction of the tomb of the prophet Hosea, great prophet of social justice, and again toward Meron, where is the mausoleum of Rabbi Simon ben Yochai, great patriot and mystic, pronouncing them not graves but halidoms, deaths invested in life. For this was such a land, he said, where out of its tombs come light as out of the lion's fell sweetness.

In that assembly where Uncle Melech's passing was being made into a dedication service, I was the only one within the degree of mourning. As at the center of a whirlwind, amidst a great silence, I intoned the kaddish for my uncle who had had no son, uttering with pride this wonderful mourner's Magnificat which does not mention death; with pride, for it was flesh of my flesh that was here being exalted. The name that had once rung for me with angel pennies was resounding now to the conning of a new alphabet. It was my kinsman's name.

Uncle Melech was brought to his final rest. The crowds dispersed. I turned for the last time from the city of Safed, holy city on whose hills once were kindled, as now again, the beacons announcing new moons, festivals, and set times.

GLOSS ALEPH

AUTOBIOGRAPHICAL

Out of the ghetto streets where a Jewboy
   Dreamed pavement into pleasant Bible-land,
   Out of the Yiddish slums where childhood met
   The friendly beard, the loutish Sabbath-goy,
   Or followed, proud, the Torah-escorting band,
   Out of the jargoning city I regret,
   Rise memories, like sparrows rising from
   The gutter-scattered oats,
   Like sadness sweet of synagogal hum,
   Like Hebrew violins
   Sobbing delight upon their Eastern notes.

Again they ring their little bells, those doors
   Deemed by the tender-year'd, magnificent:
   Old Ashkenazi's cellar, sharp with spice;

The widows' double-parlored candy-stores
And nuggets sweet bought for one sweaty cent;
The warm fresh-smelling bakery, its pies,
Its cakes, its navel'd bellies of black bread;
The lintels candy-poled
Of barber-shop, bright-bottled, green, blue,
    red;
And fruit-stall piled, exotic,
And the big synagogue door, with letters of
    gold.

Again my kindergarten home is full—
Saturday night—with kin and compatriot:
My brothers playing Russian card-games; my
Mirroring sisters looking beautiful,
Humming the evening's imminent fox-trot;
My uncle Mayer, of blessed memory,
Still murmuring maariv, counting holy words;
And the two strangers, come
Fiery from Volhynia's murderous hordes—
The cards and humming stop.
And I too swear revenge for that pogrom.

Occasions dear: the four-legged aleph named
And angel pennies dropping on my book;
The rabbi patting a coming scholar-head;
My mother, blessing candles, Sabbath-flamed,
Queenly in her Warsovian perruque;
My father pickabacking me to bed

To tell tall tales about the Baal Shem Tov—
Letting me curl his beard.
Oh memory of unsurpassing love,
Love leading a brave child
Through childhood's ogred corridors, unfear'd!

The week in the country at my brother's—(May
He own fat cattle in the fields of heaven!)
Its picking of strawberries from grassy ditch,
Its odor of dogrose and of yellowing hay—
Dusty, adventurous, sunny days, all seven!—
Still follow me, still warm me, still are rich
With the cow-tinkling peace of pastureland.
The meadow'd memory
Is sodded with its clover, and is spanned
By that same pillow'd sky
A boy on his back one day watched enviously.

And paved again the street: the shouting boys,
Oblivious of mothers on the stoops,
Playing the robust robbers and police,
The corncob battle—all high-spirited noise
Competitive among the lot-drawn groups.
Another day, of shaken apple trees
In the rich suburbs, and a furious dog,
And guilty boys in flight;
Hazelnut games, and games in the synagogue—
The burrs, the Haman rattle,
The Torah dance on Simchas Torah night.

Immortal days of the picture calendar
Dear to me always with the virgin joy
Of the first flowering of senses five,
Discovering birds, or textures, or a star,
Or tastes sweet, sour, acid, those that cloy;
And perfumes. Never was I more alive.
All days thereafter are a dying off,
A wandering away
From home and the familiar. The years doff
Their innocence.
No other day is ever like that day.

I am no old man fatuously intent
On memoirs, but in memory I seek
The strength and vividness of nonage days,
Not tranquil recollection of event.
It is a fabled city that I seek;
It stands in Space's vapors and Time's haze;
Thence comes my sadness in remembered joy
Constrictive of the throat;
Thence do I hear, as heard by a Jewboy,
The Hebrew violins,
Delighting in the sobbed Oriental note.

GLOSS BETH

ELEGY

Named for my father's father, cousin, whose cry
  Might have been my cry lost in that dark land—
  Where shall I seek you? On what wind shall I
  Reach out to touch the ash that was your hand?
  The Atlantic gale and the turning of the sky
  Unto the cubits of my ambience
  Scatter the martyr-motes. Flotsam-of-flame!
  God's image made the iotas of God's name!
  Oh, through a powder of ghosts I walk; through
     dust
  Seraphical upon the dark winds borne;
  Daily I pass among the sieved white hosts,
  Through clouds of cousinry transgress,
  Maculate with the ashes that I mourn.

Where shall I seek you? There's not anywhere
  A tomb, a mound, a sod, a broken stick,

Marking the sepulchers of those sainted ones
The dogfaced hid in tumuli of air.
O cousin, cousin, you are everywhere!
And in your death, in your ubiquity,
Bespeak them all, our sundered cindered kin:
David, whose cinctured bone—
Young branch once wreathed in phylactery!—
Now hafts the peasant's bladed kitchenware;
And the dark Miriam murdered for her hair;
And the dark Miriam murdered for her hair;
The relicts nameless; and the tattoo'd skin
Fevering from lampshade in a cultured home—
All, all our gaunt skull-shaven family—
The faces are my face! that lie in lime,
You bring them, jot of horror, here to me,
Them, and the slow eternity of despair
That tore them, and did tear them out of time.

Death may be beautiful, when full of years,
Ripe with good works, a man, among his sons,
Says his last word, and turns him to the wall.
But not these deaths! Oh, not these weighted
    tears!
The flesh of Thy sages, Lord, flung prodigal
To the robed fauna with their tubes and
    shears;
Thy chosen for a gold tooth chosen; for
The pervert's wetness, flesh beneath the rod—
Death multitudinous as their frustrate spore!—

This has been done to us, Lord, thought-lost
    God;
And things still hidden, and unspeakable more.

A world is emptied. Marked is that world's map
The forest color. There where Thy people
    praised
In angular ecstasy Thy name, Thy Torah
Is less than a whisper of its thunderclap.
Thy synagogues, rubble. Thy academies,
Bright once with Talmud brow and musical
With song alternative in exegesis,
Are silent, dark. They are laid waste, Thy cities,
Once festive with Thy fruit-full calendar,
And where Thy curled and caftan'd congrega-
    tions
Danced to the first days and the second star,
Or made the marketplaces loud and green
To welcome in the Sabbath Queen;
Or through the nights sat sweet polemical
With Rav and Shmuail (also of the slain)—
Oh, there where dwelt the thirty-six—world's
    pillars!—
And tenfold Egypt's generation, there
Is nothing, nothing . . . only the million
    echoes
Calling Thy name still trembling on the air.

Look down, O Lord, from Thy abstracted
    throne!

Look down! Find out this Sodom to the sky
Rearing and solid on a world atilt
The architecture by its pillars known.
This circle breathed hundreds; that round,
    thousands—
And from among the lesser domes descry
The style renascent of Gomorrah built.
See where the pyramids
Preserve our ache between their angled tons:
Pass over, they have been excelled. Look down
On the Greek marble that our torture spurned—
The white forgivable stone.
The arch and triumph of subjection, pass;
The victor, too, has passed; and all these spires
At whose foundations, dungeoned, the screw
    turned
Inquisitorial, now overlook—
They were delirium and sick desires.
But do not overlook, oh pass not over
The hollow monoliths. The vengeful eye
Fix on these pylons of the sinister sigh,
The well-kept chimneys daring towards the sky!
From them, now innocent, no fumes do rise.
They yawn to heaven. It is their ennui:
Too much the slabs and ovens, and too many
The man-shaped loaves of sacrifice!

As Thou didst do to Sodom, do to them!
But not, O Lord, in one destruction. Slow,

Fever by fever, limb by withering limb,
Destroy! Send through the marrow of their
bones,
The pale treponeme burrowing. Let there grow
Over their eyes a film that they may see
Always a carbon sky! Feed them on ash!
Condemn them double deuteronomy!
All in one day pustule their speech with groans,
Their bodies with the scripture of a rash,
With boils and buboes their suddenly breaking
flesh!
When their dams litter, monsters be their
whelp,
Unviable! Themselves, may each one dread,
The touch of his fellow, and the infected help
Of the robed fauna with their tubes and shears!
Fill up their days with funerals and fears!
Let madness shake them—rooted down—like
kelp.
And as their land is emptying, and instructed,
The nations cordon the huge lazaret—
The paring of Thy little fingernail
Drop down: the just circuitings of flame,
And as Gomorrah's name, be their cursed name!

Not for the judgment sole, but for a sign
Effect, O Lord, example and decree,
A sign, the final shade and witness joined
To the shadowy witnesses who once made free

With that elected folk Thou didst call Thine.
Before my mind, still unconsoled, there pass
The pharaohs risen from the Red Sea sedge,
Profiled; in alien blood and peonage
Hidalgos lost; shadows of Shushan; and
The Assyrian uncurling into sand;
Most untriumphant frieze! and darkly pass
The shades Seleucid; dark against blank white
The bearded ikon-bearing royalties—
All who did waste us, insubstantial now,
A motion of the mind. Oh, unto these
Let there be added, soon, as on a screen,
The shadowy houndface, barking, never heard,
But for all time a lore and lesson, seen,
And heeded; and thence, of Thy will our peace.

Vengeance is thine, O Lord, and unto us
In a world wandering, amidst raised spears
Between wild waters, and against barred doors,
There are no weapons left. Where now but
    force
Prevails, and over the once blest lagoons
Mushroom new Sinais, sole defensive is
The face turned east, and the uncompassed
    prayer.
Not prayer for the murdered myriads who
Themselves white liturgy before Thy throne
Are of my prayer; but for the scattered bone

Stirring in Europe's camps, next kin of death,
My supplication climbs the carboniferous air.
Grant them Ezekiel's prophesying breath!
Isaiah's cry of solacing allow!
O Thou who from Mizraim once didst draw
Us free, and from the Babylonian lair;
From bondages, plots, ruins imminent
Preserving, didst keep Covenant and Law,
Creator, King whose banishments are not
Forever—for Thy Law and Covenant,
Oh, for Thy promise and Thy pity, now
At last, this people to its lowest brought
Preserve! Only in Thee our faith. The word
Of eagle-quartering kings ever intends
Their own bright eyrie; rote of parakeet
The laboring noise among the fabians heard;
Thou only art responseful.

                              Hear me, who stand
Circled and winged in vortex of my kin:
Forgo the complete doom! The winnowed,
        spare!
Annul the scattering, and end! And end
Our habitats on water and on air!
Gather the flames up to light orient
Over the land; and that funest eclipse,
Diaspora-dark, revolve from off our ways!
Towered Jerusalem and Jacob's tent

Set up again; again renew our days
As when near Carmel's mount we harbored
    ships,
And went and came, and knew our home; and
    song
From all the vineyards raised its sweet degrees,
And Thou didst visit us, didst shield from
    wrong,
And all our sorrows salve with prophecies;
  Again renew them as they were of old,
  And for all time cancel that ashen orbit
  In which our days, and hopes, and kin, are
    rolled.

GLOSS GIMEL

EXCERPT FROM LETTER: *"On First Seeing the Ceiling of the Sistine Chapel"*

ET LEVAVI OCULOS MEOS: ET VIDI ET ECCE VIR, ET IN MANUS EJUS FUNICULUS MENSORUM.

. . . to the Sistine Chapel; and so to me the long passage through the marble corridors leading to the beatific door was no more than a flotation upon a channel of foam, a transit between walls of wind forgotten as soon as blown. The white statuary of that ghostly gantlet I recall as but a series of pale shadows, a spectral escort. I do not even remember my walking; like something dreamed in a dream of walking on water, such and such feebly the recollection of that calm wan floor. The ceiling—was there really a ceiling above these interminable candid galleries?—the ceiling even then was less than a thought, a mere scalp's awareness: and all, ceiling, floor, and walls, all vanished for me as I reached the threshold of that door and, the long umbilical cord of corridors behind me, pressed forward with infant eagerness to enter this new world, truer than sculpture, not tunneled, but global—ceilinged.

I entered, and I lifted my eyes to the cosmic vault, and scanned its expanse, paneled, pullulant, populate. Head flung back—this heaven breaks even the necks of the proud—I paced up and down the alexandrine floor, circling the chapel, casting my gaze from miracle to miracle, pursuing the arrowheads of the spandrels to each pointed particular wonder. At first I saw only geometry: triangle consorting with square, circle rolling in rectangle, the caress parabolic, the osculations of symmetry: as if out of old time Euclid were come to repeat his theorems now entirely in terms of anatomy. Theorems they are, but theorems made flesh; for at last it is not the whirlwind of forms but the tornado of torsos that abashes the little homunculus below, puny before the myriad bodies instant, ambulant, volant, who in their various attitudes and postures are turned and contorted to make of the ceiling the weighted animate corpus of humanity.

High and central in the chapel's empyrean the throned twenty bear down with an almost palpable imminence. Young men, handsome and marvelously sinewed, wonderful in their proportions, they are the prototypes of the human kind; and whether face-to-face conversant or januarial back-to-back, or in their serpentinings muscle-rippled, there is upon them everywhere the glory of God's accolade. Brooding nudities, they are themselves like gods. Long-limbed, Atlas-shouldered, lyre chested, each body is a song echoing the Creator's voice. *Fiat!* The dew of paradise is still upon them, they are ichor-fresh, ambrosia-scented; their gaze is Eden-rapt, all are adonic, almost adonaic! It is also to be seen that they know themselves earthlings, earthlings involved in concatenations far from celestial: group after group of them is perceived tangled in the circuit of those murderous medallions rolling before their feet, from which they recoil back horror-struck. Circle-racked! Caught in these wheels the color of dried blood, it is clear that they have an awareness of the ambiguity of their plight: their pristine unmarred felicity ever in peril of cicatrice and brand-mark. That peril, however, is below them, below their knees, and even there dark and obscured; about their countenances another aura reigns, the memory of the fingertouch, of God's lifegiving fingertouch, which through each pulsating vein and every quickened limb proclaims divine origins and makes of this adamic-seraphic ceiling a pantheon of gods.

This—these men writ big—this is the flesh majuscule: there are also the charming minor ones, the lesser clan springing from the heels of the giants—a stance of caryatids, a conjugation of cherubim. But the idiom of the twins and doubles—affectionate damonandpythias, most loving davidandjonathan—though not of a lordly utterance, still speaks its tribute to the divine quickness of the mortal flesh. Belly to belly, to buttock buttock, hand by thigh, and on nipples palm, it is in gross comic terms, almost in terms of parody that the mischievous pairs advert to the condition of their immortality—an itch, not an afflatus. It is out of this itch, the rub and yearning of their essence, that they fashion, like coupled philosophers, the dialogue of being. Out of upholding heaven, which is their proper duty, they make a game, these gemini in a zodiac of delight, and their tête-à-têtes are sibilant of the secrets of the universe they brace. They embrace, ambivalent bambini, and their contacts and touchings are copy, an ingratiating and pathetic imitation, of that first famous fingertouch. The ceiling sounds with their diphthongs.

The whole ceiling is indeed in all its parts and divisions, its burdens and canticles, but a tremendous pæan to the human form divine, a great psalter psalmodizing the beauty and vigor and worth of the races of mankind. It is the parable of the species that is pendent over me, and nowhere can I scan that ceiling but I must encounter my semblable and like. For four long years suffering the ordeal of the scaffold Michael Angelo—say rather the Archangel Michael—inscribed this testament, his pinion for a brush; and one sole word it was that stood him for lexicon, one word from the changes and declensions of which he phrased the Law and the Prophets: *The Flesh.* (Twelve score and eight the limbs, parts, and members of the body, and eighteen score and five its organs and sinews—the sum all-embracing of commands and forbiddings, the six hundred and thirteen, *curriculum taryag!*) In that altitude one temperature prevails—the temperature of the human body. One color dominates this ceiling—the color of living skin; and behind the coagulation of the paint flows the one universal stream of everybody's blood.

It well may be that Michelangelo had other paradigms in mind: there is much talk of *zimzum* and retractations; but such is the nature of art that though the artist entertain fixedly but one intention and one meaning, that creation once accomplished beneath his hand, now no longer merely his own attribute, but Inspiration's very substance and entity, proliferates with significances by him not conceived nor imagined. Such art is eternal and to every generation speaks with fresh coeval timeliness. In vain did Buonarotti seek to confine himself to the hermeneutics of his age; the Spirit intruded and lo! on that ceiling appeared the narrative of things to come, which came indeed, and behold above me the parable of my days.

ET EUM, QUI AB AQUILONE
EST, PROCUL FACIAM A VO-
BIS, ET EXPELIAM EUM IN
TERRAM INVIAM ET DESER-
TAM; FACIEM EJUS CONTRA
MARE ORIENTALE. ET AS-
CENDET FETOR EJUS, ET AS-
CENDET PUTREDO EJUS,
QUIA SUPERBE EGIT.   *Joel*

ET FILIOS JUDA ET FILIOS
JERUSALEM VENDIDISTIS
FILIIS GRÆCORUM.   *Delphica*

Certainly I could not look upon those limbs, well fleshed and of the color of health, each in its proper socket, each as of yore ordained, without recalling to mind another scattering of limbs, other conglomerations of bodies the disjected members of which I had but recently beheld. For as I regarded the flights of athletes above me the tint subcutaneous of well-being faded, the flesh dwindled, the bones showed, and I saw again the *relictæ* of the camps, entire cairns of cadavers, heaped and golgotha'd: a leg growing from its owner's neck, an arm extended from another's shoulder, wrist by jawbone, ear on ankle: the human form divine crippled, jackknifed, trussed, corded: reduced and broken down to its named bones, femur and tibia and clavicle and ulna and thorax and pelvis and cranium: the bundled ossuaries: all in their several social heapings heaped to be taken up by the mastodon bulldozer and scavengered into its sistine limepit.

And so that I might understand the meaning of this wreckage, the poet set between his unmaimed heroes his painted homilies of sin and crime. It may have been wine that brought old Noah to shame and uncovering; a headier liquid, as red as wine and more potent, intoxicated my generation's men of blood. This is the great drunkenness that whirls in the wheels of the medallions, of treachery smiting under the fifth rib, of bodies cast upon a plat of ground to be trodden underfoot, of carcasses diminished to scull, and feet, and the palms of the hands, of murder, murder, murder that cutteth off all life. For even as wine lifts man up a little higher than his stature, so too was the shedding of life for the sons of Belial vanity's temptation. They would be like gods; but since the godlike touch of creation was not theirs, like gods would they be in destructions. To kill wantonly, arrogantly to determine that another's term is fulfilled—with impunity to do these things and be deemed therefore gods—such were their vain imaginings, the bouquet and flavor of their drink. It was the sin against our incarnate universality. Comes then Michelangelo to teach us that he who spills but a drop of the ocean of our consanguinity exsanguinates himself and stands before heaven by that much blanched, a leper; that such beginnings have terrible ends: it is the first murder that is difficult: and that the single gout released sets cataracts of carnage on to flood.

Such were the imaginations of the thoughts of the hearts of men who denied the godliness of all flesh but their own. A survivor of the Ark, I fled the deluge of the uncontained blood; the scenes and flights that Michelangelo forecast onto this ceiling, I beheld them, I was part of them. Well has the prophet done to depict the victims in their nudity; always it was, always it is in nakedness that one meets one's fate. That fate in its hundred engulfing forms I saw; I saw the husband in flight from the mounting flood carrying his wife on his shoulders, she looking in terror back; and saw both turned to salt and chemicals. Witness was I to the father bearing his dead son to the mother that bore him, and they enduring but long enough to wish their death. Women I saw convert blessing to curse, seeking to live in their blood; they, too, perished. I was privy to the many devices of escape; the most were futile. The victims themselves I saw, fighting one another, struggling in blood, for that additional hour of survival. And of all I heard their weeping, which was drowned.

ET TIMEBUNT ET CONFUN-
DENTUR AB ÆTHIOPIA SPE
SUA.   *Erithræa*

QUO MIHI MULTITUDINEM
VICTIMARUM VESTRORUM,
DICIT DOMINUS. . . . PLE-
NUS SUM: HOLOCAUSTA. . . .
NOLUI, INCENSUM ABOM-
INATIO EST MIHI.   *Esaias*

With what sibylline intuition did the poet look forward into the dark future, there to discern the burning rituals that filled our sky with smoke! He has not been able to bring himself to paint them in their barbaric literalness; through the medallion shadowing the babes of Moloch sent into the fire and through that adumbrating the innocent man made sacrifice and put in the forefront of battle, he has hinted, he has pointed at his as yet unconflagrated meaning. Explicitness would have shriveled his palette; wherefore it is the creature animal, brute and beast, that we are offered for a burnt offering upon Noah's altar, and see Noah himself raising his index finger—the finger now blaspheming life!—to adduce the scenes before. They are all of a piece; only now it is not blood that is the tale, but the white leukemia of ash. How could this scene—this cattle issued from what cattle-cars, these sheep to slaughter led, these goats, these azazels— speak otherwise to me than of recent furnaces and holocausts? Only before those latter fires it was the human form that lay prostrate and bound, bleating; while the cornute heads readied the blade and the faggot. The horror of his own prophecy abashed him, this scene the angel would not limn; there rises, therefore, before the nostrils of Noah the incense of the fat of fed beasts. But the odor is the odor of the fume of humanity.

From flood and fire those who could flee fled. It was a flight into a limbo of neither life nor death, an expulsion from the earth nowhitherwards. This, too, out of his sæcular presentiments Michelangelo imaged upon the ceiling. It is not a paradise from which he shows expulsion: no flowers spring from

143

the earth, no lush vegetation, no crystal streams; it is a landscape infertile of barren soil and unyielding rock where no thing grows save the malefic tree on which hermaphrodite evil sits and loves itself. It is the landscape of our life on earth; no Eden, but the little to which we cling. Yet even from this little my generation was cut off.

By an angel? Not angel is he wielding the expelling sword: see! from the rib of the Serpent, like Eve from Adam's rib, he rises. They are one person. But the apple? There is no apple. In that entire frame there is no apple. There are gestures as of rondures grasped, reached, held; but there is no apple in that scene. There is only the subtil illusion of apples.

In the writ whence Michelangelo drew his moral there surely was that fruit. By what intervention, then, did it come to pass that the apple was lost from that tree, from those hands, from this the world's first parable? Design was it or forgetfulness? It was the spirit of prophecy. It was the spirit of prophecy that veiled the painter's memory and took hold of his brush and changed a chapter of genesis into the vision apocalyptic: mankind from mankind wresting the habitation of earth, by guile and by violence, and my kinsmen set forward in flight, their backs forever shuddered with pursuit. Oh, bitter homelessness that owns not even its isle of banishment!

TU AUTEM, FILI HOMINIS, VATICINARE ADVERSUM GOG, ET DICES: HAEC DICIT DOMINUS DEUS: ECCE, EGO SUPER TE, GOG. *Ezechiel*

IBI IDUMÆA ET REGES EJUS, ET OMNES DUCES EJUS . . . QUI DESCENDUNT IN LACUM. *Cumæa*

We approach now a fuller explication—an unfolding—of the ugly heinousness of killing. Like a plant growing against a wall Adam lies croziered and convolute, and from his body, at the behest of God, Eve blossoms forth. The chain of generation is thus figured; we know now, seeing Adam, seeing Eve, that man is not born for a day, but for all time; that under the guise of fecundation, immortality is symboled; and that man, being also a seed, may between his thighs compass eternity. It is murder of the codes to snap the thread of a man's life. Such homicide the sons of Belial committed in thousands of thousands, a thousand thousand for each day of the six days of creation. Alas, alas for their victims, and alas for them, that their crime did not end with this slaughter but is forever repeated and multiplied: as the constellations move in their courses and the years and decades pass and the generations that should have been born are not born, the hand that slew is seen again to be slaying, and again, and again; frustrate generation after frustrate generation, to all time, eternal murder, murder immortal! Peruse the circles circling the tableau of the risen Eve—you would not say that so idyllic a conjuration—man as one with his helpmate—should be rounded on the one hand by the house of Abner brought to naught and on the other by the prophet exclaiming: *Thou Art the Man!* Yet so it is; the deed is named: the hand of the Lord is lifted, beckoning levitation, and what horror shall be affixed to the hand that slaps His down?

Lies on the ground the body of Adam anticipative. It has its due limbs, its due members, its quantum of blood in the veins. It resembles a man. Its length is extended and curved, its arm is fixed outright, its hand hippocratic in hue hangs limp. Awaits its completion, languid, a hemisphere; awaits; and encircled by spheres and cycles of potency, robed in the draped whirlwind, the future under His cloak and all possibles in His ambience trembling, with flight of power and might of majesty, with beauty, with splendor He brings to the earthen mold recumbent His finger's imminence—oh, benedictive touch! —life, and the glory of His countenance! And in his eyes is imaged God. . . . He dared not transliterate it, Michelangelo, he dared not point the burden of his charge. But I read it plain and spell it out—summation and grand indictment—the unspeakable nefas—deicide.

EGO OSTENDAM TIBI, QUÆ
FUTURA SUNT IN NOVISSIMO
MALEDICTIONIS, QUONIAM
HABET TEMPUS FINEM SU-
UM . . . ARIES . . . REX
MEDORUM EST ATQUE PER-
SARUM.   *Persicha*

ECCE, EGO VIDI QUATUOR
VIVOS SOLUTOS ET AMBU-
LANTES IN MEDIO IGNIS, ET
NIHIL CORRUPTIONIS IN EIS
EST, ET SPECIES QUARTI
SIMILIS FILIO DEI.   *Daniel*

But deicide—its syl-
lables contradict each
other—this is the evil
possible only in its at-
tempt, not in its per-
petration. A covenant
stands between man
and his destruction, the
covenant of sea and sky:
the bow in the cloud.
Not otherwise than by
this, God's seal, were
the people spared.
Though bloody coursed
the red and orange fe-
vered bright, though the pus yellow yeasted, the
gangrene green and the smitings waxed bruise-blue
contused to indigo and the virulent violet, violet
waned, the indigo fled, the veins throbbed azure,
and green was the world once more and golden,
high sanguinary, and the body ruddy with health.
The remnant would be whole again. And that this
would come and in this wise come Michelangelo signified it, writing on a ceiling his seven-sealed token
ADAM PALSYN ZAHAV YEREQ KOHL ISOTHYS ADAM—
SAPIRI, signified it and between God's palms stablishing sea and sky preserved it. All colors melled to
hope; the spectrum fused to white.

The people endured; floated out the flood; defied the furnace. With their foretold salvation fulfilled, there revived also into existence and shone bright the worlds and planets which without man their beholder are as if they were not. The clouds vanished, and the sky was starred again; the clouds vanished, and the sun shone. Upon the breath of little children is the whole globe poised, say the Talmudists; and say: every human soul is weighted against worlds three hundred and ten. Oh, the proliferation in the heavens as the dry bones stirred! Oh, the enkindled suns the moons gilded the splendiferous satellites and the aureoled glories that sprang forth luminous, scintillant, extant! as a swooned generation opened its eyes once more to see . . .

ET REDUCAM ISRAEL AD HABITACULUM SUUM ET PASCITUR CARMELUM ET BASAN, ET IN MONTE EPHRAIM ET GALAAD SATURABITUR ANIMA EJUS. *Iheremias*

ASCENDITE EQUOS ET EXULTATE IN CURRIBUS ET PROCEDANT FORTES ÆTHIOPIA, ET LIBYES TENENTES SCUTUM.   *Lybica*

to see the Author of their Days, not in the image of man made—with what triumphant orthodoxy does Michelangelo at last in peroration doff his metaphor to breathe upon the ceiling the true concept—the form of formlessness, unphrasable, infinite, world-quickening anima, the shaped wind!

—not in any manner image, not body, nor the similitude of body, but pure pervasive Spirit intelligential, the One (oh, musculature of flame!) the First, the Last (oh, uncontainable fire unconsumed!) Cloud numinous with Creation, Omnipotent, yes, and All-Compassionate, who in the heavens resides and in the heart's small chambers (beating little heart of Isaac on the faggots . . .) magnanimous with Law, and who even to the latest of generations fulfills His prophets' prophecies, rebuking, rewarding, hastening for them who wait him who tarries, merciful-munificent with ascensions, aliyoth, resurrections, authorizing Days. . . .

Hence the illumination of the four corners squared and rounded. From east, from west, from north and south, the quadruplicate communiqué of heaven, the prophecy in four salvation scenes made clear, made eternal: not ever shall He utterly forsake! It is a covenant.

It is a covenant, here of the fourfold type, confirmed through the grace even of the young stripling who slang his one smooth stone, the shepherd's mite, to lay low and dented the six cubits and a span of Gath's Gogmagog, gigantical Goliath. Thus in the hour of challenge is Israel saved.

Or even through a female. Judith, the maid of Bethulia, who in the valley of Esdraelon rendered acephalous the headstrong Holofernes, the arrogance of Persia that henceforth at the shoulders

149

ceased. Thus in the hour of threatening is Israel spared.

Through a dream, the dream that remembered Mordecai who did remember Esther who brought to remembrance the Lord's pact, whereby the man Haman was destroyed, his design confounded. Thus in the hour of peril does Israel triumph.

And even through a fiery serpent, when that it is looked upon, and named by name. Thus in the hour of brass, thus in the round of serpents, by God's grace, Israel lives.

The sigils, talismans, and magic circles of Michelangelo to this purpose did I read; and when at last I stood beneath the sign of the gourd and whale's head, the prayer of Jonah in the fish's belly spoke for me:

> The waters compassed me about, even to the soul: the depth closed me round about, the weeds were wrapped about my head. I went down to the bottoms of the mountains; the earth with her bars was about me for ever: yet hast thou brought up my life from corruption, O Lord my God.
>
> . . . I will sacrifice unto thee with the voice of thanksgiving, I will pay that that I have vowed.

Thus did I leave the chapel, noting for the last time the series of rams' skulls of which the poet had made a device to signify, some say, descent to mortality. But to me, through the long marble corridors hurrying back, they were rams' horns, sounding liberation.

GLOSS DALID

THE THREE JUDGMENTS

BAGHDAD. The Gates of Justice. A raised, canopied dais, as yet unoccupied, guarded by four soldiers with scimitars. Before it, a concourse of litigants, chained criminals, merchants, beggars.

FIRST
BEGGAR: Allah be praised! the hungry week
has passed
And the Gates of Justice thronged again
—we thrive!
And high time! Ah, this poor purse, it
has had
A lean and constricted week,
Its strings, folded and fallow, like a gut
at Ramadan. . . .

SECOND
BEGGAR: But today it will gorge. This sweet
                 congregation of guilt
        Palsied with fear and philanthropy, it
                 will pay
        The long fast of our adjournment. And
                 they are many
        Who have need of our intercessory purse,
                 more even
        Than a week ago when this devotional
                 sack, this
        Wallet of mercy, this talisman against
                 mischance, this purse
        Ingested two hundred gold coins
        Nicked with petition, prayer, and plea.
                 There were,
        You remember, twenty acquittals.

FIRST
BEGGAR: Not to mention
        Convictions twenty-three.

SECOND
BEGGAR: Of those who wasted on others
        Allah's baksheesh. Never you lose sight
                 of the fact,
        Nor let the world forget, that to have
                 patronized the pious
        Is better than to have chosen the subtlest
                 lawyer.

The pious plead before a court the lawyer cannot enter.
How many do you think we will have
today
Who will require our eleemosynary office, accused
The soles of whose feet itch with the imminence of bastinado,
Whose napes already raise resistant hair
against the sword,
Whose hearts with the echo of justice
thunder? I go
To gather statistics. (*Looks up at the
sky.*) If it rains
We'll starve again!—For the love of Allah! alms!
Win a good judgment, alms!

FIRST
BEGGAR   [*joining in the stroll of the out-
stretched palm*]: Let the poor
Plead for your riches, and the innocent—

SECOND
BEGGAR: Argue your innocence! Alms!

[*A flourish of trumpets. Enter the* CADI.]

SCRIBE: Wisdom alights on the earth! A
week's wrongs
Are about to be mended. Let all who are
aggrieved

153

Approach the throne. The scales of jus-
tice already quiver
Toward the level of an equable equity
and the order of the world
Yearns toward our Koran. The aggrieved
Will grieve no more.

SECOND
BEGGAR: Whoever's aggrieved—I'm aggrieved,
I'm a pauper.
But should I rise up and say:
I have, O judge, a cause against the
world:
I was forgotten—when all the goods of
this good earth
Its treasures hid, and its treasures flung
On the open field, its growing, its delved
rainbows,
Its surfeiting wealth was portioned, I
was forgotten,
I was left holding a tail
Of the hamsin; and now from your wis-
dom
Ask a wherefore—
The answer is prepared: I will be told,
As if it were a lewd invitation: *Kismet!*
Blame Kismet! There is your thief, your
villain!
Oh, if in that other world I should ever
meet

This now invisible Kismet, I shall surely
    embrace him,
Receive him, cherish him in my dearest
    hiding-place,
Strangle him
With this the cord that he kept forever
    limp
Like a waterless vine.

SCRIBE: Decorum! Silence! Whoever's ag-
    grieved,
Let him come forward!

JEW: [*running forward from the fringe of
    the crowd*]: Help, Prince! Help!
I've been robbed! My jewels! My jewels!
    The velvet box,
My sky, has been cleaned out! Three
    million
Stars are missing!

[*Soldiers rush forward, hold him, resist-
ing.*]

From a prince
I have been made a scavenger, looking in
    dirt
For the pieces of my fallen heavens. O
    Cadi,

155

Somebody came in the dead of night and stole
My day away.

SOLDIER: Dogsonofadog! Turd of impudence!
Leek's reek!
You dare
To darken with your uncleanness the Ca-
di's vision! What—

SCRIBE: Let him be. He's mad. As delirious
as sand in a storm.
In the armillary sphere of his own brain
he lives, among constellations
Not yet discovered, and from time to
time pops out
To recognize the world. Let him be. A
lunatic's auspicious,
If only for one's own self-esteem.

[*Flung into a corner, the Jew rises, with dignity.*]

JEW: Mad, I am not mad. Yet is it wonderful
That in a world of madness I retain it—
Like the old coin of a broken emperor—
My reason.

SCRIBE: Whosoever is aggrieved—

ABDUL

IBN AZIZ: It is an affair between me and my
slave. In your father's day
When a slave escaped and through dogs,
hunger, or informers
Was brought back again,
His master with a nine-tongued whip
taught him
Domesticity. Now a new law applies. He
must be heard
In open court; he who would take him-
self off—and his master's property—
Must be heard and judged in open court,
lest, so it is said,
Lest cruelty, excuseless, indulge itself
On the body innocent for whom speaks
no protector.
Therefore is this slave brought that he
may be heard.
And punished.

SLAVE: Father of mercies, master of the
slave who owns this slave,
And this slave's master of masters,
O Cadi, hearkening—to efface it—the
realm's anguish
Even to hearing the whimper of the
worm—I fled
Because I would be heard.

157

ABDUL

IBN AZIZ: Let him be heard, then, counting
the strokes
Fettering his mind against a repetition,
let all slaves
Equally curious about the beyond beyond their master's walls
Hear him as well.

SLAVE: But first let the Cadi hear me,
And let the Cadi judge between me
And my brother.

ABDUL

IBN AZIZ: Brother! *Brother!* Oh, what is the
world
Coming to when the cleaners of our priv-
ies, in the midst of midden,
Rise up to call us brothers! Brother!
I a brother of this oath-loud dung-proud
lout! It is
The end of all society and the throne it-
self
When chattering chattel dare affront its
lord
With brazen vile fraternity!

CADI: You are advised to watch your language, slave.

SLAVE:　　　　　　Forgive what for the moment seems
　　　　　　　　presumptuous. Soon
　　　　　　Out of the branches of my narrative the
　　　　　　　　fact,
　　　　　　Like fruit, will fall. I was born free,
　　　　　　Descended from a line as pure, as noble
　　　　　　As my master's. The faith was with our
　　　　　　　　tribe
　　　　　　From the days when the blessed coffin
　　　　　　　　hung in the sky. . . .
　　　　　　As a gay garden bulbulating with night-
　　　　　　　　ingales,
　　　　　　Such was my childhood. . . . The last
　　　　　　　　pearl of my father's loins
　　　　　　He doted on me; I was a theme woven,
　　　　　　A flower recurrent in the khalabar of his
　　　　　　　　love.
　　　　　　And then, in my eleventh year—

ABDUL
IBN AZIZ:　　　　　　　　　　Are we to listen
　　　　　　To the story of his life?

SLAVE:　　　　　　　I was with my father's caravan
　　　　　　Winding its wealth to Basrah, silks and
　　　　　　　　gems—
　　　　　　Silks which unrolled the shot and fame
　　　　　　　　of Islam's cities,
　　　　　　Baghdad, Dameshek, Mosul, and Fustat;
　　　　　　And jewels that were like Allah's

Bright afterthoughts after the gleam of
creation.
We were traveling at night; it was my
first camel
Nodding me drowsy as the camel-drivers
Sang in the night the long and languor-
ous note
That drops like a star. . . . All of us
Were in a mirage of thought where Bas-
rah shone with palms—
When suddenly out of the darkness they
fell upon us,
Beards shouting our death, bandits re-
leasing from their robes
Damascus murder curved to the curve of
a throat!
My father—oh, I can still see his sword
flashing
Directions to heaven and see his sword
fall
As his hand fell
As bleeding he fell to damascene the
sand!
The caravan was pillaged and our men
slain.
Me, the chief of the robbers, for a fancy
he had,
Spared, kept for his slave. . . . O Cadi,
I shall not tax your pity

With the long ache of my bondage, its
 vicissitudes,
The various auction-blocks from which
 the greedy, the leering,
Raising the fingers of my price, took me
 to teach me
The aleph and tau of a master's whim,
 until at last
I was sold to my present lord.
I did not know him for my brother, nor
 he me. . . .

ABDUL
IBN AZIZ: His own admission!

SLAVE: But when I was brought to his
 house
And from the slaves' quarters permitted
 his rooms, I saw
What nullified the decades. The tall
 vases!
Had they not loomed like robed broad-
 shouldered guardsmen
Over the tiles of my nursery? And these
 divans,
Were they not of the design on which
 my eyes had wandered
Those somnolent afternoons when my
 fingers toyed with my father's beard?

Oh, all that furniture, hanging and heir-
    loom,
Yes, and my father's chessboard with lit-
    tle white elephant
Mechanic and snorting—
They whirled time back, they tore off
    from my eyes
The pus of slavery, and brought me back
A child in my father's house!
I knew then this was kinsman, and when
    later I was made
My master's confidant, keeper of his
    deeds,
I came upon it—more glorious than Su-
    leiman's seal!
My father's seal, with its device, the dou-
    ble eagle!

ABDUL
IBN AZIZ: He saw my father's seal; therefore
he's my brother.

SLAVE: I showed these things to my master,
and said
That if I were held in a far captivity
It would have been our father's will that
    he ransom me;
How much more so when I labored un-
    der his hand.

I forgave him, I said, my legacy; I only
    asked
My freedom.

CADI: I gather he did not grant it.

SLAVE: He flew into a zenith of high anger,
Fixed upon me the epithets of all mon-
    grels, kicked me,
Spat a thick spittle on me, and beat me
    to the ground.
He then ordered his boys to pick me up,
    and promised me
A promotion.

CADI: Brother remains brother!

SLAVE: He promised, seeing I was of such
close kin, of the same womb,
To promote me eunuch in his harem! He
    would frustrate
His own father's seed. I fled.
And I plead, O Cadi, for my name and
    freedom!

ABDUL
IBN AZIZ: It's true my father left me wide es-
    tates,
And true I had a brother. These are facts

Well known throughout Baghdad. May
any impostor,
Any mountebank juggler, and in especial
any slave
Made privy to our household nooks, our
family lore,
May such a one therefore come forward,
adduce me signs,
Gasp recognition, embrace me brother,
and kiss
In a brotherly rapture his brother's goods
away?
Am I, because he is mimic, and chose a
touchy role,
To reward him therefore with freedom,
and attribute him
To my chaste and saintly mother?

CADI: Slave, your cause staggers. Have you
better proof
To justify what, if unjustified, is gross
slander,
A graver wrong than your mere strolling
off?

SLAVE: I have uttered, O Cadi, not what I
wished, or feel,
But what I know. . . . As I remember
my father's face,

So I remembered the things in my broth-
er's house
That were my father's. As I hope
To look in due time on that countenance
in heaven,
So is he brother that I now look upon. O
Cadi,
If my mother stood resurrected from her
tomb,
How she would weep this day to see her
sons—
One bound, one blind!

CADI: Defense is not sustained. An exam-
               ple must be shown.
          I order that this overweening slave be
               flogged.

ABDUL
IBN AZIZ: O wise judge!

CADI: But deviate
          From the usual procedure in such case
               set and provided.
          First, in that he is to be punished pub-
               licly, and second,
          At his master's hand.

ABDUL
IBN AZIZ: And if he is, indeed, my brother!
          O Cadi, I forgive him!

CADI: The kerchief of pardon is the court's.
                         Execute sentence!

ABDUL
IBN AZIZ: I hear and I obey!

[*The back of the slave is bared and one
stroke is delivered, without outcry. As
Abdul ibn Aziz is about to strike a second time, he comes forward and scans
closely the slave's back.*]

ABDUL
IBN AZIZ: Forgive! Allah, forgive! It is indeed
                            my brother!
                         Here, but an inch below the welt, see, O
                            Cadi,
                         Our double-wingèd mole,
                         The birthmark of our tribe, my father's
                         Signature and calligraphy! I have it, too!

                              [*Reveals it.*]

                         Brother, brother, how shall I ever win
                            pardon?

                            [*Embraces him.*]

                         A slave have I lost and—Allah be praised
                            for the eloquence
                         Of our flesh—have found a brother!

SLAVE: And our father has found peace!

FIRST
BEGGAR: Did the Cadi know? There must be
an invisible bird
That sits on his shoulder and, parakeet of
heaven,
Parrots the angels, their ruses and sug-
gestions.

SECOND
BEGGAR: If so, it must have come down from
that cloud.

SCRIBE: Whosoever is aggrieved—

[*The Jew rises and would come toward
the Cadi.*]

SCRIBE: Is it the undelivered lashes that you
covet, Jew?
Away, or you shall yell Hebrew!

[*A beggar extending his arm, crying
alms, with his five fingers pokes the Jew
back.*]

HASSAN: I cite the merchant Ahmed, who
would be
My father-in-law, yet would not be.
For seven years I served him, in his gar-
dens,
And in his booth at the angle of the wall

In the Attarabiyah. His flowers flour-
    ished under my hand,
Under my skill his perfumes, spices, and
    scents
Made the air swoon. We had good cus-
    tom.
Our attars set eager the harems of Bagh-
    dad,
The unstoppering of our philters brought
    love,
Like a pollen in the month of Nissan, to
    our youth.
And for these my skills and this my de-
    votion
The merchant Ahmed betrothed me his
    daughter.

AHMED: I am ready to keep my promise. My
           daughter Zuleika—

HASSAN: Zuleika, Zuleika—forever he rings
           that name
           Like counterfeit coin; but he knows well
           It was Yasmin he promised me.

AHMED: That may be. But that was seven
           long years ago,
           And now my wife is dead, and I, an old
           man,

Bereaved and solitary, would keep Yasmin,
My oldest, so like her mother, to be my
home,
An old man's home before the last muez-
zin calls.

HASSAN: Servant-girls and maids can be
hired. Yasmin
Was promised me.

AHMED: Offering, O Cadi, for Hassan's de-
light
My youngest, Zuleika—
Like a full moon, at the fortnight, beau-
tiful—
I favor him,
Whereas Yasmin, though dear to me, is
plain,
Is not well favored, no, not ugly, plain.
Her eyes
Are eyes, like eyes in a doctor's book, her
nose
A nose, no more, her mouth for speech,
not kisses made,
And altogether one for whom no poet,
but only a father
Would bite his beard. Hassan himself,
when we struck our pact,

Bargained about the scar on her brow, the cut she had
When, a little girl, she fell
Bringing her father his cup of sherbet.

HASSAN: It is unbecoming to a father to speak thus
Of his daughter. I admit that Yasmin is older—
If that is loss, it's my loss—that there is anyone
More beautiful, I deny; but no matter
Were she as hideous as the demon Kashkash,
My heart is hers, and hers is mine.

CADI: Your two daughters, are they here?

AHMED: They are on the other side of the Gate of Justice
Waiting from a distance
The disposing of their father's last gray hairs.

HASSAN: And their own futures. O Cadi, the maid Yasmin,
Though faithful to her father, loves Hassan. I had it

Many and many a time from her own
lips.

[*Ahmed beckons to his daughters. They
enter.*]

CADI: We will have judgment and the
shining truth
Through an unveiling of veils.

AHMED: O just! O wise!
Now it will be seen whether I seek to
cheat
And spigot my bargain or seek to over-
brim it!

HASSAN: But, O Cadi, to unveil before—

CADI: Modesty is a virtue,
But less than the finding-out of justice.
The maid Zuleika will unveil.

[*Zuleika obeys.*]

A moon, at the fortnight?
The moon, compared to her, is ancient
hag!

CITIZENS: Her father's garden, surely, has no
rose
Lovelier than the roses on her face!

171

Her eyes—they were not born, they were
dreamed!

This Hassan is a fool!

Or short-sighted!

And from that face
Imagine the beauties that are not unveiled!

CADI   [*visibly impressed*]: Well—

HASSAN: She is my beloved's sister. Naturally
She is presentable.

CITIZENS: Presentable!

HASSAN: But not her sister!

CADI: Yasmin, daughter of Ahmed!

[*She approaches, unveils.*]

An old man's nurse!

CITIZENS: Not, not Zuleika!

A scar?

That's no scar, it's a wart!

Ahmed's a flatterer—he said *plain*.
Would that Zuleika stood unveiled again!

HASSAN: Is it not seen,
Is it not seen by all,
Yasmin, the most beautiful of woman-
kind!
From mother Hevah all the blossoming
generations
Have bloomed, have bettered only to-
wards Yasmin! Oh, without her
The world were total male to me! She
sets up babel
Upon a tongue that knows not which to
praise
First of her beauties, nor which of a thou-
sand
Bright similitudes would not pale
Before the paradise of her person. She
shames
My aphrodisiacs. She is the motion of
my heart.
I will not ever die as long as I look on
her.
She is my betrothed and happiness.
Grant me her,
The reward of seven seasons of turban'd
tulips
Nodding approval of our pact—and love.

CADI: We have heard, have seen, have
            meditated. That the merchant Ahmed,
            Now past the age of houris, and a wid-
               ower,
            Wishes the companionship of his oldest
               daughter
            Is understandable; but not a righteous-
               ness.
            A pledge is a pledge, a thing of honor.
            It is undesirable, further, that a daugh-
               ter of Islam
            Be kept a father's nun. Moreover,
            Love here has spoken out its love, which
               though it seem
            To eyes unloving a babbling after a mi-
               rage
            Is still the heart's locution, and will have
               sway.
            —Come, my good Ahmed, call on your
               pastry-cooks,
            Get dancers, get eye-rolling musicians,
            And set the feast that feeds posterity—
            Hassan's, Yasmin's.

HASSAN: I kiss the earth between your hands!
            This day I have won a wife, the grave
               Ahmed a son;
            Nor has he lost a daughter: Yasmin shall
               be

Always at his side, making his old age
Like a pleasant reclining among the
grasses and flowers
Of a garden that fronts the happy gate.

FIRST
BEGGAR: Alms! Alms for love! Alms for the
edict of love!

[*Hassan throws some gold coin into beggar's purse. Ahmed ignores him.*]

SECOND
BEGGAR: What did you get?

FIRST
BEGGAR: From the young man, part of a
dowry
For my own daughter, and from the old
one, a clouded countenance, and
A drop of rain.

[*The Jew rises, makes to go forward
again, is tripped.*]

SCRIBE: Whosoever—

MAROUF: I am an artist of lamps. My lamps
Have made the palaces from here to Kai-
ruwan
Illustrious. My artifacts are much sought
after.
Now, three years ago I entered into a
contract

175

With the merchant Abukir, consenting
To sell to him only of the great bazaar
The said renownèd lamps, make of Ma-
  rouf.
He, for his part, undertook
To buy only my lamps; no others; to sell
My ware only. For this
He received the said lamps at a pittance
  of their price.
But now, now I discover that he sells,
Not my lamps, but the kindled pots, the
  smudges,
Of my competitors. Mine he refuses. At
  our contract he laughs.

ABUKIR: Marouf has expounded well, with
  his *saids*, his *artifacts*.
But he has forgotten, or ignores, or never
  understood
One clause of the said contract. There it
  was stated
That I was to buy from Marouf—true,
  true—
But through his agent and steward, my
  friend Mahmad.
Mahmad was expressly named, Mahmad
  was my man; from year's beginning
To year's end I dealt only with Mahmad;
  I never saw Marouf.

I dealt with my friend, my friend made
his living thereby,
And the merchant Marouf obtained the
due worth of his lamp.
Is that not true, Marouf?

MAROUF: I do not deny, but what—

ABUKIR: Admitted, then; such was the course
of the contract that first year.
Suddenly, with the coming of the fall
and the long nights
My friend Mahmad is dismissed. And at
the souk appears
With stock of merchandise, torches,
lightnings, lusters,
A galaxy of cressets, an aldebaran of
lights,
The traveler Ibn-Amram. He, he says,
now represents Marouf.
For the sake of my friend, I turned him
from my door, saying
I still had merchandise unsold.
But the next year Ibn-Amram, too, is
among the departed.
—He must be a hard taskmaster, this
Marouf!—
And appears at the bazaar
With his new virginal candles, his eter-
nal wicks,

The steward Ibn-Yussuf. . . . My contract said Mahmad.
With him only will I deal.

MAROUF: There is some deeper reason
And this is but excuse! What difference
    does it make
Who is the steward, traveler, agent,
    hawker—the merchandise
Is ever alike, of superior quality, bearing
Sign manual of the craftsmanship!

ABUKIR: To me it is of the essence.
And even if I were perverse, such is the
    contract!
But I am not perverse, O lord, and have
    good reason.
What with bargainings, insults, and dis-
    appointments,
Not many are the pleasures of a vender
    in the bazaars;
Only one pleasure is ours: trade-talk
    with merchants;
And when that merchant is Mahmad,
Then is it continual delight, wit like a
    crackling fire,
Tales of wonder and fulgurant lamp-
    lighting tricks,
The very stars seem to be seen by day!

Oh, you should hear him, this card of a
   Mahmad,
Apply the abracadabra to his sconces
And with his sesame and hocus-pocus
Set his flame to color red, green, blue—
A rose, a grass, a star:
Wonderful, and is worth a fourth of my
   contract!

MAROUF: But the trick lies in my lamps,
Not in Mahmad.

ABUKIR: The trick—but not the language,
Not the illuminant sentence of my friend
   Mahmad,
Compared to whom Aladdin was a sitter
   in darkness.

MAROUF: This gift for palaver which Abukir
   affects to love
Is glibness of the trade—all stewards talk
   it!

ABUKIR: Not Ibn-Amram!
He was a stutterer; before he could say
   l-l-light,
The light was out! And a meek man, too,
   the meekest.

179

I didn't really have to turn him from my
    door; he turned
Himself. . . . And what demonstrations
    of lamps he made!
He would take this candelabrum of his,
    this torch,
And it would be *This you must not
    touch; this part mustn't be rubbed;
Careful with this part.*—Oh, you might as
    well leave it standing by itself
And wait for dawn. . . . And never a
    joke from him!

MAROUF: Then why complain his dismissal?

ABUKIR: Consider who followed him: Ibn-
    Yussuf, a most
Lugubrious fellow. He wasn't too bad
At selling tapers and flares and torches,
    lights
For light,
But set him to selling the articles of art
    and luxury
And his talk makes the robes of the ba-
    zaar
Flutter with laughter. This golden giran-
    dole,
He would say, is only golden, but it sheds
    a light.

"Is only golden!" Can you imagine? "Is
    only jeweled!"
Perhaps we should offer gratis a cask of
    oil
With one of those only golden, only jew-
    eled girandoles!
Dervish dips and rushes for hermits
Should have been his stock and radiance,
Not the make of Marouf!

CADI: And that is your plea and defense?

ABUKIR: I think it's enough.

CADI: It is not enough. It is immaterial
    who
The steward or agent is. The light, the
    light is—
To borrow your excellent phrase—of the
    essence.
Of the shines and phosphors of Marouf
    you have made
No complaint. It is taken that his lamps
Were in all respects satisfactory, kindled,
    and threw the light.
He, therefore, has fulfilled his part of
    your bargain.
Do you now, under the penalties of this
    court,

Fulfill yours and let no dark
Obnubilations of salesmen dim the day
Lit by your contract, which is clear, as
  though it were
A lamp, make of Marouf.

MAROUF: I bow before the brightness
Which were it vendible, as—Allah be
  praised!—it's not,
Would bankrupt me.

FIRST
BEGGAR: The cloud comes, and the darkness.
Oil for my humble lamps! Merciful peo-
  ple,
Do charity before the storm comes!

JEW: O Cadi, though your soldiers hack
  at me, and slice,
Yet will I speak, I'll plead for judgment,
  I'll—

[*Pushed and buffeted, the Jew is at last
before the dais.*]

SCRIBE: We have warned you, you have
  been twice forgiven.
How long will you abuse the privilege of
  madness?

CADI: Let him be. Let him stand. It pleases
  us

To be jewdicious. What grace, Izak,
Do you seek from us? Ask, and you shall
be given.

JEW: Your rendered judgments three!

CADI: Ah, you are a slave-owner?

JEW: No.

CADI: A lamp-lighter?

JEW [*hesitating*]: Perhaps.

CADI: But no doubt a father-in-law!

JEW: I am a Jew.
And in that quality, such as that is, I
plead,
Petitioner *and* plaintiff. A Jew: that is to
say,
One who in great Baghdad is—far from
home.
An exile, stranger, slave, a thing, a thing
Polluted! A Jew: that is to say, one dis-
regarded,
Or regarded, tripped and mauled, in-
vested

[*Draws himself up to full stature*]

With Baghdad's honorific medals, its ex-
pectorations.

183

My crime? Annunciator of the world's
    first fidelity,
Infidel am I deemed!

CADI: You need not tell us
What a Jew is. We know only too well.

JEW: Since, then, you are a knowing
    judge, and a just,
And since the hour is late and the rain
    threatens,
I would not impose further meditations
    on your wisdom.
Grant me what is already rendered:
The equity of your most exemplary de-
    cision:
Of Abdul ibn Aziz his judgment!

CADI: How? How is that?
Ibn Aziz? Ah, he has a mole! And you,
You are all mole and splotch; therefore,
    a fortiori—
Is that your reasoning?

JEW: Admit to brotherhood a brother!

SCRIBE: This fraternity, it's a contagion in
    the land!

JEW: For we are consanguine of blood!
The syllables of Shem conjoin our
    speech.

184

In the tents and under the tamarisks of
olden time
We descry them, our bearded and robed
uncles,
Mine, yours. Oh, of the same sire de-
scended,
Are we not all one kin, one tribe, one
race?
Arrayed in identical splendor, or in sim-
ilar tatters,
Who can tell us apart?
Naked, we are to the last member and
limb,
To the very wound of religion,
Alike, alike, alike!
Onto your face as onto mine
Has our Father Ibrahim, with the gener-
ations for mirrors, cast
The cast of his countenance!

CITIZENS: The arrogant Jew!
O long-suffering Cadi! For my part, I
would smite him down
To crawl beneath the belly of an ant.

JEW: You are bound, therefore, O Cadi,
by your own decree—
My freedom.

CADI:　　　　You have already had much freedom
In speech. Is there anything else you'd
like?

JEW:　　　　My home, my country, that in sub-
jection lies.
It lies in ruins and is desert, but to me,
to us,
Is still oasis, green Jerusalem!
It's my Yasmin, my first love, and though
marked and pocked
With the seventy diseases brought from
far
Is still more beautiful than all earthly
vision.
No, not Euphratic song nor praise of Ti-
gris
Can steal my heart
Away from the banks of Jordan where it
dreams.
It dreams a wedlock—the wedlock of
Hassan.

CADI:　　　　Oh, this goes beyond all humor!
The very sky darkens at such impudence.
One wonders how it can be excelled.
You spoke, Jew,
Of a third judgment?

JEW: The judgment of Marouf!
          What is it stands between us? Not disbe-
               lief!
          We worship all the same great sovereign
               Lord;
          In gesture and genuflection differ,
          Differ only in the choice of him we send
          With our soul's embassy to the throne of
               God;
          In all other respects we do not differ.

               [*Some heavy gouts of rain fall.*]

          Is ours, then, not the case of Abukir?
          For hear, O Cadi, there is but one God!
          His is the light, the one transcendent
               light

          [*The storm breaks; thunder and light-
          ning accompany the Jew's peroration.
          The Cadi cowers beneath his canopy.*]

          Illuminating the dome of heaven and
          The little alcoves of the private heart.
          His prophets and vicars, porters of His
               flame,
          Announce the light—but theirs is not the
               light.
          The light is God's! That light sees all. It
               sees

The wicked hiding behind the cloak of
the prophet,
The innocent oppressed, and justice
dazed
By its three flashes into remainder dark-
ness.
O Cadi, lest judgment fall upon you,
Grant it, the triple justice: the recogni-
tion of kinship;
The love restored; and acknowledged the
one light!
Hassan, Marouf, and Ibn-Aziz—they
were but proxies;
I am your plaintiff! I demand their judg-
ments
Here in the sight of God and in the hear-
ing
Of His most angered voice. Heed it, O
Cadi!
Heed it, the thunder of your conscience,
And overcry it with brother, still it with
freedom!
Let lightning enlighten! Let this thun-
der thunder
Understanding! Let . . .

[*Curtain.*]

GLOSS HAI

Who hast fashioned:

Blessed art thou, O Lord,

Who in Thy wisdom hast fashioned man as Thou hast fashioned him: hollowed and antrious, grottoed and gutted, channelled; for mercy's sake gifted with orifice, exit, and vent!

Did one of these only suffer obstruction, survives not the hour that man!

Thy will according, there drops the baneful excess: the scruff falls; from the pores surreptitious the sweat; and the nails of the fingers are cut; the demons are houseless.

Be blessed for the judgment of the eight great gates who dost diminish us to make us whole; for the piecemeal deaths that save; for wax and cerumen, which preserve all music, and for flux of the sinus, which gives the brain coolness, its space,

189

and for spittle prized above the condiments of Asia;
even for tears.

Benedictions:

For that he gave to a stone understanding to under-
stand direction.
For that he made no slave for me.
For that he clothes the naked with the nudities of
beasts.
For that he erects the contracted.
For that he smites me each dawn with a planet.

Grace before poison:

Well may they thank Thee, Lord, for drink and food;
For daily benison of meat,
For fish or fowl,
For spices of the subtle cook,
For fruit of the orchard, root of the meadow, berry
of the wood;
For all things good,
And for the grace of water of the running brook!
And in the hallelujah of these joys
Not least is my uplifted voice.

But this day into Thy great temple have I come
To praise Thee for the poisons Thou has brayed,
To thank Thee for pollens venomous, the fatal gum,

The banes that bless, the multifarious herbs arrayed,
In all the potency of that first week
Thou didst compose the sextet of Earth spoken,
    made!

Behold them everywhere, the unuttered syllables of
    Thy breath,
Heavy with life, and big with death!
The flowering codicils to Thy great fiat!

The hemp of India—and paradise!
The monkshood, cooling against fever;
And nightshade: death unpetaled before widened
    eyes;
And blossom of the heart, the purple foxglove!
The spotted hemlock, punishment and prize,
And those exhilarators of the brain—
Cocaine;
Blood of the grape; and marrow of the grain!

And sweet white flower of Thy breath, O Lord,
Juice of the poppy, conjurer of timeless twilights,
Eternities of peace in which the fretful world
Like a tame tiger at the feet lies curled.

Of remembrance:

Go catch the echoes of the ticks of time;
Spy the interstices between its sands;

Uncover the shadow of the dial; fish
Out of the waters of the water-clock
The shape and image of first memory.

Recall:
The apple fallen from the apple tree:
O child remembering maternity!

The candle flickering in a mysterious room:
O fœtus stirring in the luminous womb!

One said he did remember, he did know
What time the fruit did first begin to grow:
O memory of limbs in embryo!

Another did recall the primal seed—
Conceiver of conception of the breed!

A third, the sage who did the seed invent—
O distant memory of mere intent!

Recall the fruit's taste ere the fruit was fruit—
Hail memory of essence absolute!

Recall the odor of fruit when no fruit was,
O Spirit untainted by corporeal flaws!

Recall the fruit's shape ere the fruit was seen,
O soul immortal that has always been!

192

Said one, and he the keenest of them all:
No thing is what I vividly recall—
O happy man who could remember thus,
The Mystery beyond the mysterious.

Stance of the Amidah

O Lord, open Thou my lips; and my mouth
shall declare Thy praise:

God of Abraham, God of Isaac, God of Jacob,
who hast bound to the patriarchs their posterity and
hast made Thyself manifest in the longings of men
and hast condescended to bestow upon history a
shadow of the shadows of Thy radiance;

Who with the single word hast made the world,
hanging before us the heavens like an unrolled scroll,
and the earth old manuscript, and the murmurous
sea, each, all-allusive to Thy glory, so that from
them we might conjecture and surmise and almost
know Thee;

Whom only angels know
Who in Thy burning courts
Cry: Holy! Holy! Holy!
While mortal voice below
With seraphim consorts
To murmur: Holy! Holy!
Yet holiness not know.

Favor us, O Lord, with understanding, who hast given to the bee its knowledge and to the ant its foresight, to the sleeping bear Joseph's prudence, and even to the dead lodestone its instinct for the star, favor us with understanding of what in the inscrutable design is for our doomsday-good;

Oh, give us such understanding as makes superfluous second thought; and at Thy least, give us to understand to repent.

At the beginning of our days Thou dost give— oh, at the end, forgive!

Deem our affliction worthy of Thy care, and now with a last redeeming, Redeemer of Israel, redeem!

Over our fevers pass the wind of Thy hand; against our chills, Thy warmth. O great Physician, heal us! and shall we ailing be healed.

From want deliver us. Yield the earth fruitful. Let rain a delicate stalk, let dew in the bright seed, sprout ever abundance. Shelter us behind the four walls of Thy seasons, roof us with justice, O Lord, who settest the sun to labor for our evening dish!

Thyself do utter the Shma! Sound the great horn of our freedom, raise up the ensign of freedom, and gather from the four corners of the earth, as we do gather the four fringes to kiss them, Thy people, Thy folk, rejected Thine elect.

Restore our judges as in former times restore

our Judge. Blessed art Thou, O Lord, King, who lovest righteousness and judgment.

Favor them, O Lord, Thy saints Thy paupers, who do forgo all other Thy benedictions for the benediction of Thy name.

Oh, build Jerusalem!

Anoint Thy people David!

Our prayers accept, but judge us not through our prayers: grant them with mercy.

Make us of Thy love a sanctuary, an altar where the heart may cease from fear, and evil a burnt offering is consumed away, and good, like the fine dust of spices, an adulation of incense, rises up.

Oh, accept, accept, accept our thanks for the day's three miracles, of dusk, of dawn, of noon, and of the years which with Thy presence are made felicitous.

Grant us—our last petition—peace, Thine especial blessing, which is of Thy grace and of the shining and the turning of Thy Face.

And in that drowning instant:

And in that drowning instant as
the water heightened over me
it suddenly did come to pass
my preterite eternity

the image of myself intent
on several freedoms

               fading to
myself in yellowed basel-print
vanishing

          into ghetto Jew
a face among the faces of
the rapt disciples hearkening
the raptures of the Baalshem Tov
explaining Torah

             vanishing
amidst the water's flickering green
to show me in old Amsterdam
which topples

           into a new scene
Cordova where an Abraham
faces inquisitors

           the face
is suddenly beneath an arch
whose Latin script the waves erase
and flashes now the backward march
of many

        I among them

            to
Jerusalem-gate and Temple-door!

196

For the third time my body rises
And finds the good, the lasting shore!

For the Day, Psalm the Thirtieth:

I will extol thee, O Lord; for thou hast
lifted me up, and hast not made my foes to re-
joice over me.

O Lord my God, I cried unto thee, and
thou hast healed me.

O Lord, thou hast brought up my soul from
the grave: thou hast kept me alive, that I should
not go down to the pit.

Sing unto the Lord, O ye saints of his, and
give thanks at the remembrance of his holiness.

For his anger endureth but a moment; in
his favor is life: weeping may endure for a
night, but joy cometh in the morning.

And in my prosperity I said, I shall never
be moved.

Lord, by thy favor thou hast made my
mountain to stand strong: thou didst hide thy
face, and I was troubled.

I cried to thee, O Lord; and unto the Lord
I made supplication.

What profit is there in my blood, when I
go down to the pit? Shall the dust praise thee?
shall it declare thy truth?

Hear, O Lord, and have mercy upon me: Lord, be thou my helper.

Thou hast turned for me my mourning into dancing: thou hast put off my sackcloth, and girded me with gladness;

To the end that my glory may sing praise to thee, and not be silent. O Lord my God, I will give thanks unto thee for ever.